Ginnie's Baby-sitting Business

(Original Title: Ginnie and Her Juniors)

by CATHERINE WOOLLEY

Illustrated by Liz Dauber

SCHOLASTIC INC.
New York Toronto London Auckland Sydney

No part of this publication may be reproduced in whole or in part, or stored in a retrieval system, or transmitted in any form or by any means, electronic, mechanical, photocopying, recording, or otherwise, without written permission of the publisher. For information regarding permission, write to William Morrow & Company, Inc., 105 Madison Avenue, New York, NY 10016.

ISBN 0-590-04449-4

Copyright © 1963 by Catherine Woolley. This edition is published by Scholastic Inc., 730 Broadway, New York, NY 10003, by arrangement with William Morrow & Company, Inc.

12 11 10 9 8 7 6 5 4 3 2 1   6 7 8 9/8 0/9

Printed in the U.S.A.   08

Contents

Baby-sitting

"And," said Geneva, stepping carefully over a crack in the sidewalk, "Mr. Gordon said I could play the piano for marching into assembly real soon."

"Good," Ginnie said.

Ginnie and her best friend, Geneva, were sauntering home from school this September afternoon. Sunlight, slanting through tall maples along the suburban street, turned the leaves to green gold, and the air felt lush with summer's warmth.

"Wouldn't it be horrible if I made a mistake!" Geneva added.

"You won't," Ginnie assured her. "You've been taking music lessons forever." She was silent for a moment. "Are you going to be a musician when you grow up?"

"I might," Geneva said carelessly.

A car passed them, and Lucy Ransom waved at her classmates from the front seat. They waved back. "Lucy's going to art school in New York Saturdays. Did she tell you?" Geneva remarked.

Ginnie nodded. "She's wonderful in art." She shook her head ruefully. "I'm awful in it."

"She has talent. Mrs. Johnson told her she had. Come on in," Geneva invited, changing the subject as they paused at her front walk.

Ginnie shook her head. "No. I'll see you tomorrow."

She often stopped at the Porter house on the way home from school. She and Geneva had been best friends for a long time. But today she wanted to get home. She was conscious of a vaguely troubled feeling, and she wanted time to figure out what was bothering her.

She walked on slowly, thoughts remote. She passed a neighbor, Mrs. DeGraw, walking her boxer Zabriskie, and said, "Hello, Mrs. DeGraw," scarcely knowing that she had seen them.

Here was her own block, and here was the house, with its trim green lawn and bushes. Ginnie went up the steps and pushed open the door. Honey, the blond cocker, greeted her with enthusiastic wiggles.

"Oh, I know!" Ginnie paused to stroke his head. "You tell that to all the girls!" Honey shook himself happily and followed her into the kitchen.

"Hello, dear." Mother was mixing a cake, and she looked up as Ginnie came in.

"Hi."

"Did you have a good day?"

"It was all right." Ginnie put her books on the table and opened the refrigerator door. She got out a carton of milk and reached into the cupboard for a glass and a box of cookies.

Mother paused for a moment in her stirring, to follow her daughter's movements. She drew two cake pans nearer and prepared to pour the batter from the bowl, scraping it from the sides with a wooden spoon.

"Anything bothering you?" she inquired casually.

"No." Ginnie pulled a chair to the table and sat down with her milk. And then the thing that was troubling her boiled up and over in a single question. "Mother, have I got any talent?"

Mother looked up in surprise, then carefully finished pouring her batter. She scraped the bowl and shook the cake pans gently. "What brings that up?"

It was a relief to talk about it. "Well," Ginnie said, and drank some milk, "Geneva can play the piano and she's going to play for marching into assembly. And Lucy is going to art school in New York Saturdays, because Mrs. Johnson says she has talent. But I can't play the piano, and I'm terrible in art, and *I* haven't got *any* talent!"

"You never wanted to take music lessons," her mother reminded her.

"I know I didn't. I like music," Ginnie explained, "but I just don't want to play the piano. And I don't want to take art lessons. But" . . . her troubled eyes sought her mother's for help . . . "haven't I got *any* talent?"

"You can cook."

"*That's* a talent?"

Mother laughed. "It's a very useful art."

"Geneva isn't any good at cooking," Ginnie reflected with some satisfaction. She thought of Anna, the foster cousin who lived with Grandma. "Anna can sew real well."

"I'd be delighted to teach you to sew," Mother said.

Ginnie sighed deeply. "I don't like to sew either."

"Well, I wouldn't worry," Mother told her. "The important thing is to have lots of different interests. You'll probably develop some talent that you don't suspect at all right now. Incidentally," she added, "there's going to be a sale at the church. I thought you might like to make some fudge for the candy table."

"I will." Ginnie's thoughts were still on her problem. "May I go to the sale?"

"Yes, you might find some little things for Christmas presents."

Christmas seemed years away on this sultry September day, but suddenly a new problem sailed across Ginnie's horizon. "I wish I could earn some money to buy Christmas presents," she remarked gloomily.

She rinsed her glass. There seemed to be nothing to gain at this point by further considering the matter of talent, so she dismissed it. She scooped up Mumbo, the little black cat, who instantly began to purr with a deep-seated joy, and settled herself with a book in the big chair in the living room. It was Friday, and homework could wait.

Mother's fresh lemon-jelly cake was so good that both Ginnie and her father took a second piece at dinner. "That's really cake!" Daddy remarked, passing his plate.

"Thank you," Mother said modestly. She threw a sidewise glance at Ginnie. "My talent," she murmured, and they both giggled. Daddy inquired what the joke was.

"Just something between us girls," Mother informed him, and suddenly, for no reason, Ginnie felt lighthearted again. She played Scrabble with Daddy after dinner and forgot her problem.

Saturday morning was gloriously warm, although the pungent odors of crumbling foliage were creeping into the air. Ginnie went over to Geneva's. Geneva was practicing as she rang the bell, and the sound of the piano woke troubled thoughts again.

"Hi!" Geneva greeted her. "I just finished practicing. Oh, Ginnie, I want to show you the most adorable thing!" She led the way into the living room and picked up a small box from the table. "Don't tell my mother. She's upstairs. I'm going to give her this for her birthday."

The gift was a bracelet and earrings of blue stones that caught the flash of the sun as Geneva lifted them from the box. Ginnie gasped. "Oh, they're beautiful!"

"They cost two dollars. I saved my allowance. They're for when she goes out to dinner," Geneva explained happily.

"I wish I had a bracelet like this!"

"We're not grown up enough," Geneva pointed out.

"I mean just to look at." For as she gazed at the lovely trinket, a desire to possess beautiful things swelled into Ginnie's heart. Suddenly she returned the bracelet to the box and looked at Geneva with decision. "We ought to earn some money," she said.

"O.K.," Geneva agreed. "What for?"

"Lots of things. I'd like to buy some beads. You know, the long kind."

"So would I."

"And if we could earn some money," Ginnie went on, warming to the idea, "maybe we could even go to New York some time — just you and I — and go to a museum or something."

"We could save our allowances and go."

But there was this newborn wish for funds of her own, to spend on luxuries of her choosing. "I'd like to earn some," Ginnie repeated. "How can we?"

Geneva wrinkled her brow. "Baby-sitting?"

They gazed at each other. Ginnie was an only child, and so was Geneva. They had had little or no experience with babies. Besides, they were only eleven.

"Most kids who baby-sit are older," Ginnie said.

Geneva was not easily daunted. "We could try, couldn't we?"

And hope sprang up in Ginnie too. "Yes!" she cried. "Let's! I know, Geneva! If we offered to sit together, that might make up for not being older."

"Good idea," Geneva agreed. "And we could charge lower rates. Most kids get seventy-five cents an hour. We could charge fifty."

"You get twenty-five and I get twenty-five," Ginnie agreed.

"And if we could stay three hours and get a couple of jobs a week, that'd be good!" Geneva said with satisfaction.

Suddenly Ginnie was burning for action. "Let's go out now and try and find some jobs!" she cried. "I know! In the block below my house there are a lot of people with little children. Let's go there."

They set out with high hopes. Mrs. West, in the first house, was home, and received their offer of service politely. She had a small baby, and she had a sitter, she said. But she was glad to know they were available in case of need.

"The Frasers live in the next house," Ginnie said, as they went up the walk. "They just moved here."

Mrs. Fraser's small daughter Susan was three. She came to the door behind her mother, peering around her skirt with big brown eyes. Susan had red-gold hair and pink cheeks, she was chubby and adorable, and Ginnie fell in love at first sight. Susan, however, retired to the other side of the room and rejected advances.

"You two are awfully young, aren't you?" Susan's mother said doubtfully, looking from one to the other.

"That's why we're going to baby-sit together," Geneva explained.

"And only charge fifty cents," Ginnie added.

"You couldn't come at night," Mrs. Fraser protested.

The girls looked at each other. "We could come after school, if you wanted to go shopping," Geneva pointed out. "And Saturdays. Sundays too," she added hopefully.

"It's mostly at night that I need a sitter," Mrs. Fraser said, "but I'll remember you two."

They told themselves she really meant it, even if she did think them young. Both girls left their telephone numbers.

"Oh, Geneva," Ginnie said, as they came out of Mrs. Fraser's house, "isn't that Susan adorable?" She glanced back and waved, as a small auburn head promptly retreated from the window.

They made several other calls, and Ginnie went home with soaring spirits. She poured out the morning's venture to Mother. "So if any woman calls up about baby-sitting, you say we'll come!"

It was hard to concentrate on schoolwork that

week, with a possible first baby-sitting job looming. Ginnie hurried home each day hoping that a phone call might have come. But the days passed, and there was no summons to baby-sit. Gradually the excitement dimmed, the reality faded, and Ginnie's grandiose ideas of an independent income retreated. She adjusted herself for the time being to living on her allowance.

The school year was getting under way now. Ginnie worked hard at homework. Geneva played for marching into assembly with never a stumble. Ginnie admired and envied, and the worry over having no talent herself returned to plague her.

She made fudge and attended the church sale with Mother. There was a jewelry table, and she fingered the pretty ornaments longingly. She wished she could buy them all, to have and to admire. Why, she thought impatiently, doesn't *somebody* ask us to baby-sit!

Then one day the call came. Mother opened the door when Ginnie came home from school. "Mrs. West has to go out unexpectedly, and she'd like you to wheel the baby in his carriage while she's gone."

Ginnie couldn't believe it. "Oh, I've got to call Geneva!"

"Be quick about it. I told her you'd be over as soon as you came in."

Geneva arrived at Mrs. West's on the run soon after Ginnie got there. "I won't be gone more than an hour," Mrs. West told them. "Bobby's asleep. I'll put his carriage out, and you just walk up and down and around the block if you want to."

Ginnie wheeled the carriage first, feeling it her right, as the baby's mother had seen fit to call her instead of Geneva.

"Now let me, Ginnie," Geneva said. They took turns, block by block. The small West boy slept peacefully in his fuzzy blue blankets, one curled pink fist aloft.

"Isn't he darling?" Ginnie murmured, adoring.

"I wish he'd wake up," Geneva complained. "I think I'll give him a poke."

"No!" Ginnie said. "He might cry."

"It's no fun when he's asleep!"

They began to attract attention as they walked. Lucy came down the street and paused for an explanation. She admired the baby, and Ginnie began to enjoy an important feeling.

Peter Ladd, who lived next door to Ginnie, came by on his bicycle. "Whose kid?" he shouted.

"Sh!" Ginnie admonished. "You'll wake him up. And he's not a kid, by the way. He's a little baby boy, and we're baby-sitting him."

"Looks like baby-walking to me," Peter returned cheerfully.

"Want to see him?" Geneva cried.

"Nope." He was off.

"Boys!" Geneva said disgustedly.

"Oh!" Ginnie's eyes were on the baby. "You did wake him up, shouting. Oh, isn't he the sweetest thing!" She stopped the carriage. "Hello!" she said softly, as the baby's wondering blue eyes gazed solemnly into hers.

"Oh, he's a sweet darling lamb!" In her affectionate enthusiasm Geneva leaned over the carriage and put a hand on the baby's blanket. "Kitchy, kitchy, koo!" Geneva cried, chucking the baby under his chin.

That was an affront to the darling lamb. His mouth turned down, his eyes screwed up, fists flailed, and suddenly Bobby was crying piteously.

"Now you've scared him!" Ginnie cried. "There, darling; there, darling!" She rocked the carriage gently.

"Give him something to play with." Geneva picked up a rattle tied to the carriage and shook it before the infant's eyes. The indignant cries only grew louder.

"No, let's just walk. And I know," Ginnie said suddenly, as an inspiration struck her. "Let's sing.

Singing puts babies to sleep." She began to sing softly as they moved along with the carriage. "Rock-a-bye baby, on the treetop . . ."

Geneva joined in, and they walked slowly on, singing together, eyes on the small unhappy bundle waving its arms in the carriage. And gradually, as the soothing sound and motion reached him, the crying stopped, eyelids drooped, and the junior Mr. West drifted into dreamland once more. He was still asleep when his mother returned.

"Oh, thank you both so much," Mrs. West said. "You girls saved my life. Come on in while I pay you."

She gave them sixty cents instead of fifty. "It's not much when you split it," she said.

Ginnie ran home in seventh heaven, bursting into the house.

"How did it go?" Mother asked, coming downstairs to hear her report.

"Just marvelous!" Ginnie was so thrilled and excited she danced around like a top. "Oh, that baby is the most precious thing! She gave us sixty cents. Oh, he's the sweetest thing! He only cried when Geneva tickled him. Mrs. West said we saved her life. And she also," Ginnie cried, "said she might call us again! Oh, I hope she calls tomorrow!"

Afternoon with Susan

GINNIE'S JUBILATION over her baby-sitting prospects proved premature. The days passed and there were no more calls. It was the third week in September now. Her homework well under control, Ginnie was growing restive.

"I don't see why some woman can't go to the dentist!" she grumbled, sitting at the kitchen table over milk and cookies again.

Mother was making applesauce today. The sharp sweetness of the cooked apples filled the air, and Mother was straining the steaming sauce into a yellow bowl.

"You and Geneva are rather young for baby-sitting," Mother commented. "That probably has something to do with it. And neither of you knows a thing about little children. I think a mother would hesitate to leave a small child with you."

"But both of us would go!"

Mother shook her head, laughing. "Do you think two zeros in experience add up to more than zero?"

"Oh!" Ginnie flapped her hand. "We could do it."

But Mother's remark had planted a seed of doubt, and after a minute Ginnie said practically, "Well, if they don't want us to come there, why can't I bring babies — and little children — here? You'd be home."

Mother's spoon suspended in air. "I'm not looking for a job, thank you!"

But the idea was growing. "Oh, Mother, please let me tell people I can bring their children here! Just afternoons. It won't be very often. And I'll really be the baby-sitter, honest I will. You won't have to do anything! Only their mothers'll feel all right about it if they know you're home."

Mother sighed deeply and went back to work on the soft apple pulp. "I warn you I am not keen about this."

Ginnie jumped up to throw her arms around her. "Oh, you are the darlingest, sweetest, angel mother! I adore you!"

"Go along with you," Mother said.

Ginnie did go along, popping a last cooky into her mouth. "I'm going down to see Mrs. Fraser. I just adore her little girl. I'd adore to bring her over here! See you later."

She went down the street, half running, half skipping, once more filled with eager optimism. This idea would work. This time she really was on the right track.

Mrs. Fraser was home, and this time Susan did not seem quite so shy. She came out from behind her mother and gazed solemnly at Ginnie.

Ginnie said, "Hi, Susan." Instantly Susan concentrated her gaze elsewhere.

"Pay no attention to her," Mrs. Fraser advised. "She has to get to know you."

"Well, anyhow," Ginnie said, getting down to business, "I came to see you again, because I had a new idea. My mother says I can baby-sit at our house afternoons. And she'll be there, so the children will be perfectly safe even if I" . . . she hated to admit her own incompetence, but she might as well face it . . . "I mean, even if I don't know too much about children. I'd ask Geneva to come too. So if we play with Susan and do everything she wants to do, it ought to be all right."

Susan's mother still looked doubtful. Ginnie had a further inspiration. "We'll take Susan free! Just as an experiment, I mean," she explained. "Because we'll be learning too, and it would help us get started."

Mrs. Fraser laughed. "Oh, you'll learn!" she exclaimed. "You have no idea what you'll learn. You'll be a sadder but wiser girl after you've spent a few afternoons with Susan."

"I don't mind," Ginnie said stoutly, "if she can just come."

"Well, suppose we try it out," Susan's mother said. "I've got some shopping to do tomorrow. I was going to take her along, but it would be much easier if I went alone. Suppose I bring her over at three — is that when school is out? We'll see what happens."

Ginnie jumped to her feet. "Oh, thank you, Mrs. Fraser! Oh, I'm so happy!" She turned toward Susan impulsively, wanting to hug the little girl, but checked herself. "I won't pay too much attention to her," she said. "I might scare her."

"That's the idea," the child's mother agreed. "Take it easy and be matter-of-fact, and you'll get along."

"See you tomorrow then!" Ginnie cried, and once out of the door, she raced for home, excitement winging her feet.

It turned out that tomorrow was Geneva's music-lesson day. She was annoyed.

"Oh," Ginnie said in dismay, as they walked to school, "I never thought of that. But I couldn't help it anyway, Geneva. Mrs. Fraser said today. I can manage Susan alone — I think. You can be there next time."

"O.K., you can break her in." Geneva recovered her cheerfulness.

"I have to figure out what to play with her," Ginnie said.

Susan and Mrs. Fraser were in the living room with Mother when she came in from school. "Here's Susan," Mrs. Fraser said. "I'll go along. She understands she's to stay. I'll be back soon, Susan. You be a good girl and stay with Ginnie."

She left hurriedly, and Ginnie stood face to face with her first charge. "She's all yours, dear," Mother said, and retreated toward the kitchen. "Take her upstairs."

Ginnie had prepared for this moment. "Would you like to come up in the attic, Susan," she said, "and dress up in some shoes with high heels?"

That did it. The miracle happened. Susan considered for a moment. Then she nodded her red-gold head, wordlessly put her hand into Ginnie's, and allowed herself to be led up the stairs. Ginnie was speechless too. She couldn't believe her experiment was successfully launched.

There was an old bureau in the attic, filled with discarded grown-up dresses, shoes, handbags, and scarves of Mother's, from Ginnie's own dress-up days. "Now let's see." Ginnie dropped the child's hand to open a drawer. "Let's find a pair of shoes you would like to wear." She rummaged. "How about these? Or these?" She held out two pairs, flat-heeled loafers and high-heeled black-suède pumps.

A plump finger pointed to the suède pumps.

Ginnie smiled. "I thought you'd like those. Now you sit down on the chair and I'll put them on for you."

Susan sat down and held out a foot, studying Ginnie's face as the latter untied her small stubbed brown shoes. "I like you," she said, after due consideration.

Ginnie paused in surprised pleasure. "Do you, Susan?" she cried. "My, but I'm glad!"

Instantly she saw that she had been too enthusiastic. Susan withdrew. "I don't like you *much!*" she announced severely.

Ginnie felt deflated. Still, she had gained some ground. "Oh, that's all right," she said, tugging at the second shoe. "I like you very much. There you are. See if you can walk."

Susan clumped about the attic with evident satisfaction. "Now," Ginnie went on happily, "we'll find a dress-up dress!"

They picked a flowered silk, torn but vivid, and Ginnie fastened the skirt about Susan's waist. "I'll get some pins and pin it up, so it just reaches the floor." She was enjoying this just as much as Susan obviously was. She ran downstairs for pins and then turned up the skirt.

"There you are. Oh, you look adorable, Susie!" she cried. This time Susan did not flinch from her enthusiasm. "Is there anything else we could put on you? Let's look." Ginnie peered into the bureau drawers again. Susan, looking too, pulled out a yellowed lace curtain. "Oh, that's what I used to wear when I played bride," Ginnie exclaimed. "Do you want to be a bride, Susan? Look, you put this on your head, and you can put it over your face too, if you want to."

Susan wanted to. In the flowered costume, with the lace curtain drawn over her small rose-petal face, skirt turned up, and shoes clutched in one hand, she permitted Ginnie to lead her carefully, a step at a time, down the attic staircase.

Mother had been definite about the baby-sitting's being carried on above stairs. "We'll go into Ginnie's room," Ginnie said, falling unconsciously into the

manner of grownups talking to small children. "How would you like Ginnie to read you a story?"

"Yes."

But after a few pages of "The Three Bears" she became restive. "Mommy come," she announced.

Ginnie saw need for quick action. "Would you like a cooky?" Susan nodded. "You stay right here for one minute, and I'll go get some."

She ran down to the kitchen. "I need some cookies," she announced breathlessly to Mother, reaching for a box.

"What's she doing?" Mother asked.

"She's all dressed up in that old flowered dress. She looks just darling. Oh, and she said" — Ginnie giggled — "she said she liked me but" — she lowered her voice — "she didn't like me *much!*" Overcome with joyous mirth, Ginnie put her hand over her mouth and doubled up with laughter, Mother joining in.

That was why they failed to hear the small feet, high-heeled shoes kicked off, following Ginnie down the carpeted stairs.

Ginnie heard her as she reached the front hall, and hurried in. Face shrouded by two thicknesses of lace curtain, Susan was groping her way into the living room. Ginnie tried to reach her. But she was too late. Straight into a small lamp table walked Susan.

The big china lamp rocked, eluded Ginnie's outstretched hands, and toppled onto the floor with a crash.

Ginnie gasped, "Oh, Susan!"

But Susan pulled the curtain from her head and stood there, so little, so at the mercy of grownups, so round-eyed and startled at her own mishap that Ginnie could say no more. Before she even picked up the lamp she knelt and put her arms about the little girl. "It's all right, honey," she said.

"I didn't mean to," Susan assured her.

"Of course you didn't."

Mother was picking up the lamp. "It isn't broken. Just the reflector, and that can be replaced. Well, Susie-Q," she said, "you'd better wear that veil down your back instead of your front!"

"Off," ordered Susan, throwing the veil aside and coming to Ginnie to have her dress unbuttoned.

That simple act of faith was all Ginnie needed. This small human being was hers to serve, to safeguard, and to comfort. Oh, I just adore her, she said to herself. But she carefully refrained from alarming the little girl with a hug as she unfastened her dress. "Now step out. There you are. Now you're Susan again instead of a big lady."

"Go home," Susan announced.

Ginnie's eyes flew to her mother. It was only four o'clock, so there was an hour to fill. "Why don't you walk over to the store with her?" Mother suggested. "There are several things you can get for me."

Susan went willingly. But inside the supermarket she rejected Ginnie's offer of a ride in the grocery cart or the privilege of pushing the cart, and went off on an exploration of her own. Ginnie kept an eye on her, leaving the cart several times to locate her charge. Susan inspected the cooky shelves, with which she was clearly familiar, and Ginnie caught up with her in time to save a pile of boxes from tumbling. Susan had extracted a box of animal crackers. A few minutes later, when Ginnie went in search, she found her scattering packages of gumdrops.

"Susan, you stay with Ginnie!"

Susan trailed along obligingly.

"Hello, Ginnie," a voice said. Ginnie looked up to see Mrs. Porter pushing a cart. She paused with her own and failed to notice her small charge disappear busily around a corner. "I thought you were baby-sitting today," Geneva's mother said.

"I am. I mean I was." She looked around. "I mean I still am, only I'm — well — baby-shopping, I suppose. Susan is around here some place."

"How are you making out?"

"Oh, fine! Tell Geneva Susan's an angel! She's good as gold. She did have one little accident, but she didn't mean to. Only the reflector of the lamp got broken."

Mrs. Porter raised her eyebrows. "Is that all? Well, good!"

It was then that Ginnie suddenly became aware that something about the store was different. Puzzled, she looked about.

"What happened to the lights?" Mrs. Porter asked in surprise.

That was it — the lights had gone out. "I don't know," Ginnie said. Then she noticed an odd stillness. After a moment she realized that in the meat department, near which they were standing, the meat grinder had stopped working. Up front, where several lines of customers waited at cashiers' counters, the cash registers were silent.

"The electricity is all off," Ginnie said. And with the words a premonition seized her. "Where . . . ?" she said. She left her cart and hurried toward the front of the store. Where was that child? Ginnie crossed the store, glancing down each lane.

Then she saw the rear of a small figure. It was bending over in an obscure dark corner and, as Ginnie approached, the figure stood up and sauntered toward her.

Ginnie and the store manager bore down at the same time. "Susan," Ginnie said, "did you . . . ?"

"She must have turned it off," the manager said, heading for the fuse box in the corner.

"Did you turn off the lights?" Ginnie was incredulous.

Susan nodded agreeably.

It was on the tip of Ginnie's tongue to say, "You naughty girl!" But with Susan's small soft hand in hers she couldn't. Susan was too little. Susan had no idea what she had done. She couldn't scold her for the result of an innocent investigation. It was my fault, she thought, for not keeping her right with me. "I'm terribly sorry!" she gasped to the manager, and hustled her charge away without further ado.

And as she stood in a long line of delayed and annoyed customers, Ginnie felt hot with embarrassment, but she was also seized by an almost uncontrollable desire to burst out laughing. She was obliged to cough loudly to conceal the laughter that would not stay down.

She was vastly relieved to get out of the store. "Susan," she said, her voice wavery with mirth in spite of her efforts to sound grave, "you must never, never, never do that again! Will you remember?"

"Yes," said Susan.

I'm absolutely going to burst if I don't laugh, Ginnie thought. She clenched her teeth and almost choked. And then they met Mrs. DeGraw and Zabriskie.

"Hello, Mrs. DeGraw!" Ginnie cried. "See, you're walking Briskie and I'm walking Susan. Ha, ha, ha!" She laughed so heartily that Mrs. DeGraw looked at her oddly, and even Susan stared. But Ginnie had got the giggles out of her system; she felt better.

Mrs. Fraser was waiting for them. "Did you have a good time, darling?" she cried.

"Yes."

"What did you do?"

An inquiring glance at Ginnie. Three-year-olds can't remember what they have been doing. "You dressed up, remember?" Ginnie told her. "And"— she almost mentioned the broken reflector but decided against it — "we read a story and went to the store."

"Went to store."

Mrs. Fraser gave a sigh of relief. "That's wonderful. You may have a steady customer, Ginnie."

"Oh, that's good!" Ginnie said.

Susan's mother opened her bag. "This was to be a free experiment, but I'm going to pay you. Fifty cents an hour, you said, and she was here two hours, so here's a dollar. I got twice as much done as I would have if she'd been trailing along."

"Thank you very much!" Ginnie said in pleased surprise.

"Say good-by to Ginnie," Mrs. Fraser said.

"'By."

"Are you coming back, Susan?" Ginnie asked longingly.

"Tomorrow."

"Maybe not tomorrow," Mrs. Fraser corrected. "But soon."

Ginnie watched the little girl down the walk and into the car before she turned toward her mother with a huge and happy sigh. "Oh, I didn't tell you what she did in the store!" she said, remembering. "She was just awful! I almost died, I was so embarrassed. She opened the door where the electric switches are, and turned something, and all the electricity went off. Everybody was mad, only it was so *funny*. . . ."

"And highly dangerous!" her mother said severely. "It's a good thing you didn't tell her mother. Heavens, Ginnie, you must hold on to her every minute!"

"Don't worry," Ginnie said, sober again. She had learned a lesson.

Suddenly she dismissed the disturbing incident from her mind, and her face broke into an ecstatic smile. "Do you know what I want when I grow up, Mother?" she demanded.

"What?" Mother asked, smiling in sympathy.

"Twelve children!" cried Ginnie.

Tommy Comes Too

THE SUMMER WARMTH lingered on, the lovely September afternoons filled with enveloping sunlight. Ginnie was walking home with Lucy Ranson today, as Geneva had hurried home for her music lesson.

"Did I tell you I started art lessons?" Lucy asked.

"No, did you?"

"Yes, and they're just wonderful. I go every Saturday. And after class my mother and I have lunch, and then we go to a museum. Have you ever been to the Guggenheim Museum?"

"No."

"It's real modern," Lucy said. "But since I've had art lessons I can understand it a little."

Ginnie said nothing, but she thought about art, and she felt inferior. She mentioned it to Mother. "Lucy goes to a place in New York called the Guggenheim Museum. Did you ever hear of it?"

"Yes."

"Could we go there some time?"

"If you'd like to."

Perhaps, Ginnie thought, there was some secret about art that, if she learned it, might at least make it possible for her to talk to Lucy. Lucy's art lessons and museum trips, like Geneva's music, made her vaguely uncomfortable, because they were another world to which she had no key and could not enter.

So the very next Saturday Ginnie and Mother took the big brown express bus into New York and rode a Fifth Avenue bus to the Guggenheim Museum. Ginnie looked about the rotunda with curiosity. But when they had taken the elevator up and had started down the long curving ramp, lined with strange, unintelligible paintings, she stared at them, unbelieving. "It looks like what you do in kindergarten!"

"Not exactly," Mother said.

"But they aren't pictures of anything. I thought art was pictures of people and country and stuff like that."

Mother gave her a little lecture on color and proportion and other aspects of modern art. Ginnie listened doubtfully.

"Well, I could paint that!" She pointed to a canvas, consisting of interlocking black squares against a blue background. "I just can't draw — a banana!"

"We might get some books from the library," Mother suggested, "and see if we can find out something about modern art."

They were back in the rotunda now. "Why don't we go to the Metropolitan Museum of Art as long as we're here?" Mother said. "We can have lunch in the restaurant and look around."

Ginnie liked the quiet, serene restaurant, with its tables set about a placid pool of water. Afterward they walked through galleries hung with paintings of easily recognizable subjects. She liked some of the portraits of people, and she stood entranced before canvases riotous with the colors of summer gardens. "I wish we had this one!" she breathed.

But museums, she decided, made her feet hurt. She was glad to climb onto a bus and sink into a seat.

"Have you had enough art for one day?" Mother asked, smiling down at her.

Ginnie nodded wearily. "Plenty." She had confirmed, at least, that the house with the locked door was not for her. "I'd just as soon read a book about art if it explains that modern stuff," she said. "But I never, never would like it well enough to take lessons, like Lucy, even if it was only splashing on paint!"

Her mind dwelt on the subject during the trip home, as she gazed out at the Jersey meadows. Music and art definitely were not her cup of tea. She must look for her talent, if she had one, elsewhere.

It was a few days later that Ginnie came home from school to a surprise. "See what I've got!" Mother said, as she opened the door.

Susan was there, and with her was a small boy. "His name is Tommy Poore," Mother explained. "His mother's a friend of Mrs. Fraser's, and they decided on the spur of the moment to go off somewhere. So they're all yours, dear! Take them up to your room."

Ginnie threw down her books and hastily shrugged off her jacket. "Hello, Susan and Tommy. Did you come to see Ginnie? Do you want to go upstairs with me?"

They preceded her obediently, one step at a time. I wish I could get Geneva, Ginnie thought nervously. But I can't very well leave them to telephone. Unprepared for their visit, she had to think quickly. "Here's my Teddy bear," she told them, taking her worn old bear from his place on her pillow.

This was a mistake. Susan said, "Mine," and Tommy forcibly removed it from her. Whereupon Susan's mouth quivered and she gave the young man a sound slap, which he promptly returned. Ginnie separated them hastily.

"Now we're going to read a funny story," she announced.

Tommy, it developed, was a better listener than Susan. Susan listened patiently to one story, but when Ginnie hopefully began a second she reached over and firmly closed the book. Tommy promptly lay down on his stomach and kicked. Ginnie drew him into her lap, and Susan edged in, doing her best to displace him. She was jealous, Ginnie realized suddenly. Ginnie had been hers first. This gave Ginnie a kind of pleasure, but it did not make the baby-sitting job easier.

But suddenly Susan appeared to have a change of mind and slipped away from Ginnie's arm. "I am Mrs. Bobbin," she announced, and trotted over to a corner, where she appeared deeply engaged in conversation.

Ginnie took advantage of her occupation to give Tommy the Teddy bear to hold. Then Tommy pulled the book down and began to turn the pages, telling himself the story. Ginnie watched for a while, then went quietly over to Susan. "Hello, Mrs. Bobbin," she said.

Mrs. Bobbin ignored her and went on mumbling to herself.

Ginnie supposed she should let well enough alone, but she couldn't resist trying to communicate with this Mrs. Bobbin. She reached out and knocked on the wall. "Knock, knock. Are you home, Mrs. Bobbin?" she called.

No reply. Ginnie didn't know what made her do it, but she reached out again and, this time, knocked gently, twice, on Susan's — or Mrs. Bobbin's — forehead. Mrs. Bobbin paused, surprised, considered a moment, and recognized her presence.

"Why, hello, Mrs. Bobbin. I thought you weren't home."

"I not Mrs. Bobbin."

"Who are you?"

"Susan. Let's play Mrs. Bobbin again. You knock." She presented her forehead and Ginnie knocked. "Boy too," Susan said.

"Do you want Tommy to be Mr. Bobbin?" Ginnie asked.

"*Mrs*. Bobbin."

"Both of you Mrs. Bobbin?"

Susan nodded. She trotted over, leaned over Tommy, placidly turning pages on the floor, and knocked twice on his forehead, an insult which Tommy promptly resented.

Ginnie explained quickly. "Susan doesn't mean to hurt you. She just wants you to play Mrs. Bobbin, and you have to be knocked on the head to be Mrs. Bobbin. Is that right, Susan?" Susan nodded. Ginnie was relieved that she was catching on. "Don't you want to play Mrs. Bobbin, Tommy?" she asked.

"*No!*" Tommy indicated his displeasure by rolling on his stomach, legs flying.

"Shall I read you another story?" Ginnie cried. "*No!*"

But now Susan picked up the Teddy bear and hurled it across the room.

"Why, Susan!"

Susan was in tears, sobbing heartbrokenly.

"What's the matter? Tell Ginnie."

"He — has — to be — Mrs. Bobbin till I — knock!"

"Oh! Well, knock then. Tommy," Ginnie shouted over the tumult of his kicking feet, "you don't have to be Mrs. Bobbin! Just let Susan knock and you won't be any more. Come on, Susan, you can knock." She knelt by the little boy, patting his back soothingly, while the knocking was accomplished.

"Now it's all right. You aren't Mrs. Bobbin. You can sit up."

By the time Tommy was restored to an upright posture and Susan's tears had stopped flowing, Ginnie felt that a change of pace was called for. "I know what," she said. "You haven't seen my kitty. I'll get her and we'll dress her up like a baby. Would you like that?"

It appeared that they would, agreeing for once, so Ginnie ran downstairs to where the little black cat lay curled in the sunshine of the living-room window. She carried her, warm and soft, back to her room, gathered doll clothes from a drawer, and sat down to dress the cat in a white dress and bonnet. Mumbo sat meek and unresisting. Ginnie giggled, pulling a limp black paw through a sleeve. "She thinks she can't move when she's dressed up. Isn't that funny?"

Mumbo got them through fifteen minutes, but it still lacked half an hour of five o'clock, and Ginnie racked her brain. Finally she thought of hide-and-seek, possible with such little children even in this one room. First Susan was induced to hide her eyes, then Tommy, while Ginnie hustled the other child behind the door, into the closet, under the bed.

At a quarter of five she decided to call it an afternoon, and conducted them downstairs to get their coats on and wait for their mothers. She glanced back at her room as they left it. Rugs lay askew, a chair had been overturned, her bed was rumpled where Tommy had hidden under the afghan. The floor was strewn with books and Mumbo's discarded wearing apparel. Children did mess things up, she thought.

She managed to say nothing, going downstairs, when both children firmly pressed smudgy fingers against the painted wall. Two sets of fingerprints marched all the way down. Mother would not be happy about that.

Downstairs, both children suddenly went wild, rushing into the dining room and around the table in the excitement of escape from the confines of one small room.

"Careful!" Ginnie shouted, as Tommy clutched the tablecloth in his circuit and pulled it halfway off. She rescued the candlesticks and hastily pushed the cloth back in place before she pursued her charges through the dangerous area of the living room, where tables and lamps lay in the path.

They acted possessed. Suddenly they were a team, arrayed against authority in the person of Ginnie. Giggling and panting, they bore down on the kitchen, where Mother suddenly blocked the way and circled both children with her arms.

"Five o'clock madness," she remarked to Ginnie. "Now you two calm down and get your coats on. Your mommies will be here any minute."

Fortunately, at that moment the mommies did appear. Both children hurled themselves into parental arms, instantly forsaking Ginnie. That was quite satisfactory to Ginnie, for once.

"They were just fine. Well, they got a little tired of sitting still, I guess, so they were chasing around," she told Mrs. Fraser and Mrs. Poore.

"I think you're a wonder," Mrs. Fraser said. She looked about and glanced questioningly at Mother. "They didn't tear the house apart?"

"Not quite," said Mother with a smile.

"Did you have a good time, Tommy?" his mother asked. Ginnie held her breath. He had cried and kicked and slapped and been slapped. How could you tell how a child would respond? But he nodded as if there was no question at all.

"Will you come again, Tommy?" she asked. Another nod. So that was all right.

She watched them all down the walk. Then she turned toward the kitchen, where Mother was starting dinner, and threw herself into a chair.

Mother looked up with a little smile. "That was quite a workout, wasn't it!"

"Oh, it was all right."

"I think one at a time is plenty for you to handle," Mother remarked. "I thought they were going to wreck the place."

"I'll keep them in my room next time," Ginnie assured her hastily. Not even to Mother would she admit that the effort of keeping two little children occupied for two hours really had strained her resources. But she thought back over the afternoon, and it seemed to her she was much wiser than she had been when she came home from school. "Children don't stick to anything long, do they?" she said.

"They have a very short span of attention."

Span of attention. She understood that now. They could sit still to listen to one story, but not to hear two. You had to give them something else to do then. Yes, she knew more about children than she had two hours before.

Then she thought of Mrs. Bobbin, created and dispelled by two knocks on the head, and chuckled. How silly, but how seriously Susan had felt about it. Tommy couldn't just turn into Tommy, once she had made him Mrs. Bobbin by knocking. He had to be changed back to Tommy by having his head knocked again. This ritual seemed all-important to Susan. Ginnie filed the curious game of make-believe away for future use.

Fudge for Sale

IF GINNIE APPEARED to be making some headway with her baby-sitting project, Geneva was not. Geneva had missed out now on two jobs, and she was disgruntled. She expressed her dissatisfaction as she and Ginnie sat idly on the Porter front steps one Saturday morning. It was October now, but still the sun burned hot in the intense blue sky.

"I don't know why everybody calls you!" Geneva complained.

"Everybody doesn't. I've only had those two jobs."

"Well, nobody calls me up."

"I wanted to have you help, Geneva," Ginnie said apologetically. "Only the first time you had a music lesson, and the second time I just didn't know ahead."

"It's not your fault," Geneva conceded.

"You ought to go see some people who live near you about baby-sitting," Ginnie advised. "I'll go with you if you want me to."

Geneva idly bounced the ball she held in her hand. "I don't know whether I want to or not. I've got another good idea for earning money."

"What?"

"You know, in magazines, you see ads for selling Christmas cards?" Ginnie nodded. "Well, I think I'm going to sell some. I sent a dollar for a sample assortment. You go around and show samples and take orders, and you earn just stacks of money. Fifty dollars!"

"How do you know everybody will buy them?" Ginnie asked practically.

"Doesn't everybody send Chrsitmas cards? They have to buy them some place."

It did sound like an easy way to make a fortune. "Maybe I'll get some too," Ginnie said. "But I won't go to any houses you go to," she assured Geneva hastily. She still wanted to do baby-sitting, but it would take a long time to earn fifty dollars that way. Indeed, she could do both. She could sell

Christmas cards while waiting for the baby-sitting business to come in.

A few days later Geneva made excited signs in school that she had news to impart. At recess she said, "My Christmas cards came. Can you stop this noon and see them?"

Ginnie walked home with her at lunch time, and Geneva proudly removed the cover from the box and displayed the cards. "There they are!"

The top card was a garish display of poinsettias. Thinking of the subdued and beautiful cards her mother always selected, Ginnie eyed it in doubtful silence.

"Don't you like them? Look at all the others." Geneva spread a dozen varieties about on the table.

"Mm. . . ."

"What's the matter?"

"I guess they're all right," Ginnie said slowly. "Only, well, I think they're kind of . . . well . . . not very pretty."

"Maybe some aren't." Geneva eyed them with a more critical gaze. "This one isn't bad."

"Not too. But I don't want to sell Christmas cards like that."

"Maybe I won't either." Suddenly Geneva swooped them up, and she seemed relieved. "I can send these myself. I didn't lose any money. I'll have to think of some other project, that's all."

"I wish we'd get some baby-sitting," Ginnie said wistfully.

"Me too. I could have kids here, the way you do at your house."

"Your mother might not like it," Ginnie cautioned. "My mother isn't too crazy about it. They get finger-prints all over the wall and crumbs around and nearly break things."

"I'm going to think of some other idea," Geneva decided once more.

Another idea did occur to Geneva a few days later. She was leaving Ginnie's house late one after-noon when Peter, going by with his paper bag over his shoulder, hurled a folded newspaper at the steps and waved a salute at the girls. Geneva paused as Ginnie stood in the open door. "Why do boys always have paper routes?" she demanded. "Why couldn't girls? Hey, Peter!" she shouted. "Wait a minute."

Ginnie stood at the door while Geneva went out to speak to him. They held a few moments' conversa-tion, and she came back. "I asked him how we could get a paper route," she said. "He told me we could go and see Mr. George at the newspaper of-fice."

"I don't want a paper route!" Ginnie cried.

"I'd just as soon. Boys who have paper routes make millions of dollars. Come with me, anyway?"

They called on Mr. George the next day, but this prospect, too, proved a mirage. Mr. George said he had never had a girl apply for a route before, and he thought probably there was a rule against it, if not a law. Anyway, the paper was not in need of any carriers. The girls left, Geneva disgruntled again, Ginnie relieved.

"You couldn't carry a great big bag of papers, Geneva."

"I could too. Look," Geneva said, changing the subject, "here comes Miss Wilson — she lives next door — and that adorable dog!"

They quickened their pace to meet the pair. "Hello, Snuffy," Geneva said, holding out her hand to the dog. He sniffed it, tail wagging.

Miss Wilson obligingly waited. "He likes you girls, don't you, Snuffy?"

"He loves Geneva," Ginnie said, looking on as the dog cavorted about Geneva, waving his front paws and puffing his warmly affectionate breath in her face.

"I love him!" Geneva declared, her arms around the dog's neck.

"We must get on with our walk," the dog's mistress said finally. "Come on, Snuffy. We have to have our walk."

Ginnie and Geneva parted in front of Ginnie's house. "Let me know if you get any real good ideas," Ginnie called out.

But it was Ginnie herself who had the next one. This was Friday night, and after the dinner dishes were washed she was restless. She didn't feel like reading or watching television. "Mother, can I make some fudge?" she said.

"If you want to. There's a bag of walnuts in the cupboard."

Ginnie cracked the nuts and cut them into bits. She mixed sugar and milk, added a lump of butter and chocolate, and stirred the mixture gently on the range. It came to a boil, bubbling gently. She turned down the gas and drew cold water in a cup to test the liquid. A delicious fragrance of rich chocolate rose to her nostrils.

"My, that smells good!" Mother said, coming into the kitchen as Ginnie scooped a bit of soft chocolate out of the cold water and put it on her tongue.

"It's done." Ginnie turned off the gas, added vanilla and nuts, and began to beat.

It was after she had poured the thickening mixture and was scooping out the soft, warm fudge left in the pan and licking the spoon dreamily, that she had the inspiration. After a minute she went into the living room, fudge pan and spoon still in hand.

"Mother, why couldn't Geneva and I make fudge and sell it?"

Mother considered. "Would you make any money?"

"Why not?"

"Well, try it and see."

Daddy put down his paper and gazed at his daughter. "Why this mania for making money? Don't we feed you enough?"

Ginnie giggled. "Yes, only we want some extra. You know, to buy jewelry and go to New York some time and . . . well, we just want to have some money, that's all. I'm going to call Geneva and ask her if she wants to sell fudge."

As usual, Geneva was receptive. "We can make it here," she offered. "Come on over tomorrow and let's make some."

This was agreeable to Ginnie. Mother endured the baby-sitting, but it might be just as well to carry out the new venture at Geneva's house.

She arrived at Geneva's the next morning, and they sat down to organize their project. "We have to buy butter and sugar and chocolate and milk," Ginnie said. "I brought some money."

"I think Mother's got all those things." Geneva went to the foot of the stairs and called to her mother. "Have we got everything to make chocolate fudge?"

Mrs. Porter came down. "I think so. But if you're going to make a profit on this fudge you may pay me for what goes into it, thank you."

"Oh well, we might as well buy our own stuff," Geneva decided. "Mother, I just happen to be a little low. Will you please lend me some money?"

"Get my bag," said Mrs. Porter.

They went to the store and bought five pounds of sugar, chocolate, butter, a two-quart carton of milk, and vanilla. "We need nuts," Ginnie said.

"Let's make half of it with marshmallows," Geneva suggested.

They invested in nuts and marshmallows, and returned laden. By now it was lunch time. Ginnie phoned her mother to say she was staying to lunch, and Mrs. Porter gave them bowls of soup and sandwiches.

Then they got down to the serious business of fudge making. They cracked nuts, and Mrs. Porter said, "Kindly sweep up the floor when you're through."

"I'll measure," Ginnie said. "Now keep still, Geneva, or I'll get mixed up." Together they silently counted the cups of sugar and milk that went into the pan. "There." Ginnie gave a sigh of relief. "Now chocolate and butter."

They took turns stirring and testing and eating the soft, half-cooked morsels. It thickened at last, and Ginnie beat the mixture until her arm was tired, then passed the pan to Geneva. Geneva almost overdid it, and Ginnie rescued the mixture and poured it in the nick of time.

"Let's eat just one piece," Geneva suggested, eying the fudge hungrily.

"We have to make sure it's good!" Ginnie pointed out, and they giggled as Ginnie sampled the nut fudge and Geneva tasted the marshmallow. Then Ginnie tried the marshmallow variety and Geneva tried the nut fudge. They decided it was salable.

There was the problem of how to package their product. Mrs. Porter suggested making up small packets in sandwich bags. "People are more apt to buy a small amount."

So a row of neat packets lay on the kitchen table. "How much are we going to charge?" Ginnie inquired.

Geneva looked at her mother. "How much?"

"You'll have to figure that out."

"How?" Geneva frowned.

"You figure out how much it cost you to make the fudge. Then you add something for profit."

Geneva got a pencil, and they began the laborious job of figuring. "The sugar was fifty-one cents," Ginnie said. "The butter was seventy-two. The milk . . ."

"But we've got some of everything left," Geneva reminded her.

"The gas cost something," Mrs. Porter pointed out. "But I'll contribute that to the cause."

"Oh, thank you," Ginnie said.

Finally Geneva threw down her pencil. "I can't figure it out. Let's just charge twenty-five cents a package. That will be. . . ." She figured. "Three dollars. A dollar fifty apiece."

They spent what was left of the afternoon peddling the homemade fudge. They encountered little resistance. Everyone seemed willing enough to pay a quarter for a bag of still-warm fudge. But making the calls took a long time. It was close to the dinner hour when they got back to Geneva's.

"All sold," Geneva announced triumphantly to her mother, waving a purse full of money.

"Good," Mrs. Porter said. "Incidentally, I washed your dishes."

Ginnie recalled suddenly the messy collection

they had left in the kitchen. "Oh, we forgot," she said apologetically. "We'll wash them the next time." But she did not relish the thought of cleaning up all the utensils each time they had finished their project.

She grew thoughtful, as she sat gazing at the dollar bill and small change in her hand. "You know what, Geneva?" she said. "We worked all day and we've only got a dollar fifty apiece. And we have to pay our mothers back. I can earn that much in three hours, baby-sitting, and there isn't any mess — except for fingerprints and crumbs, that is — and it doesn't cost anything."

"*When* you get baby-sitting jobs," Geneva pointed out.

Ginnie had to admit that qualification. "The fudge was your idea," Geneva reminded her.

"Oh, I know," Ginnie said.

But when she left to go home there was tacit agreement between them that making and selling fudge involved a great deal of work and a questionable margin of profit. Saturday was the only possible time they could do it. Ginnie did not want to back out, but she had reservations now, not considered earlier, about spending every Saturday, all day, on a fudge project. Anyhow, she thought, fingering the earnings in her pocket as she walked home, Geneva probably wouldn't want to do it again when she had thought it over.

At dinner she told Mother and Daddy about her day. "Is there anything else we could make?" she asked wistfully, holding out her plate for more meat loaf. "I mean anything you don't have to do arithmetic for?"

"Good experience," Daddy said. "I used to have arithmetic problems like that when I was a kid. 'If Ginnie and Geneva buy ten pounds of sugar at a dollar and four quarts of milk at twenty-eight cents a quart and a pound of butter at seventy cents, and make it into fudge, and if they sell their fudge at three dollars a pound, how much profit does each girl make?' "

"Oh, be quiet." Ginnie giggled and flapped a hand at him. "And, anyhow, we don't charge three dollars a pound. I wish we did." She buttered a piece of warm roll and gazed at it reflectively halfway to her mouth. "Maybe I could sell rolls. Remember what good rolls I made that time, Mother?"

"You made wonderful rolls."

"If Ginnie bought ten pounds of flour," began Daddy, "and two pounds of — what do you put in bread, lard? — and a dozen eggs . . ."

"No, thank you." Ginnie reconsidered quickly. "I won't sell rolls. Anyhow, rolls take even longer to make than fudge."

She dismissed fund raising from her mind over Sunday. But Geneva, apparently, was still mulling over ideas. She came up with a new one on Monday.

"I saw an ad about selling cosmetics — you know, toilet water and bath powder and things like that. I think I'll try it. Want to?"

Ginnie opened her lips to acquiesce, she was so used to doing whatever Geneva wanted her to. Then, suddenly, she closed her mouth. Just as suddenly, she realized that she had made her decision.

"No," she said. "I don't like to sell things. What's the use of doing something I just don't like to do?"

"Then how are you going to earn money? You want to earn some."

"Baby-sitting," Ginnie said firmly.

"We can't earn it baby-sitting. You know they want older kids who can sit at night."

That was the difficulty. "I know," Ginnie said. "But I'm somehow going to get more kids in the daytime. I don't know how. And you don't have to help if you don't want to. But I'm going to!"

Operation Attic

An uneventful week passed. No further baby-
sitting came Ginnie's way, nor did any inspiration
on how she might attract customers. Then, Sunday morning, she awoke with an idea in her mind.

Through the open window flooded the ripe sunshine of October, and heat, hissing gently in the radiator, curtained the crisp air. Ginnie rolled over,
eyes on the yellowing boughs of the maples, then
turned back to gaze thoughtfully at the ceiling.

Suddenly she was eager to pursue the plan of action that had presented itself while she slept. She sat
up, swung her feet off the bed, and reached for bedroom slippers.

Daddy was at the breakfast table when she went

down. Through the kitchen door came the welcoming aroma of coffee and muffins, and Mother looked in to say, "Good morning, dear."

"Hello, punkin," said Daddy.

"Good morning." Ginnie slipped into her chair, still blinking a little. Mother came in with the scrambled eggs. "Mother," Ginnie said, "can I go up in the attic and get down some of my old toys — the little table and the rocking horse — and have them in my room? So when I baby-sit, the children will have things to play with?"

"Why not?" Mother said, going back for the muffins. "They're just sitting up there."

"I'll get them down for you," Daddy offered.

"Oh, thank you." Ginnie attacked her breakfast happily. When she had had three muffins and had examined the funny paper, she was anxious to depart for the upper region. She hesitated in flight, surveying the table.

"No, you don't have to dry the dishes," Mother said, reading her mind. "Go along and look up your toys before you get dressed for Sunday school."

Ginnie ran upstairs, made her bed, and slipped quickly into shorts and jersey for the attic expedition. She found the rocking horse back under the eaves, where he had waited patiently for years. She pulled him out. He was minus a little paint, but fairly clean, because Mrs. Justesen, the cleaning woman, gave the attic a going over now and then. Ginnie stroked the coarse brown mane lovingly. She found the small table and its companion chair, shabby but sound.

It was pleasant in the attic this morning. Sunlight came through the three windows, and the sun's heat on the roof lent a comfortable warmth. A fly buzzed drowsily about a windowpane. It was a good attic, almost a room, empty except for the toys, a couple of trunks, and the chest of drawers where the dress-up clothes were stored. Ginnie liked the feeling of remote quiet, and she stood enjoying it.

Suddenly she looked about with new purpose, as another idea darted across her thoughts. Why take the toys down? Why not bring the children up here? She thought, the idea gaining, I could have a kind of nursery. I could easily have several children up here.

Objections intruded mildly. Would Mother be enthusiastic? How would she find several children who could come? She dismissed these questions impatiently. If she could just create such a wonderful play place that children would be eager to come, and their mothers eager to have them . . . Oh, I can, I can, I will! Ginnie thought. She turned to hurry downstairs.

Daddy, comfortable with the Sunday paper, looked dubious. Mother heard the plan in silence.

"Oh, please, can't I?" Ginnie begged. "Oh, Mother, the only way I can get little kids to sit with is to do something special! I can make a real good nursery up there. I'll take my doll carriage up and some books. Geneva'll help me. Please, please! Then it won't upset the house. And it won't bother you. And if their mothers know it won't bother you, they'll be willing to let them come. But you'll be right downstairs, so it will be all right."

"You can't always count on my being home."

"You could go out the days Mrs. Justesen's here! She's got grandchildren. She won't mind being in charge."

Daddy chuckled behind the sports news, and Mother laughed. "Mrs. Justesen doesn't know she's being put in charge of a day nursery."

"May I?" Ginnie persisted.

At last Mother said, "If it's so important, dear, try it. Just remember that you are very young and very inexperienced to run a nursery. But Mrs. Justesen can help you clean the attic tomorrow, and you fix things the way you want them. Then if you can figure out some way to attract trade, we'll see how things go."

Ginnie gave a great sigh.

"This will be your problem entirely, Ginnie," Mother warned her. "I have no intention of being a baby-sitter, remember."

"Oh, I know it's my problem!" Ginnie agreed gladly.

She wasted no time in briefing Geneva on this latest grandiose scheme. Geneva was her partner and must be included. And Geneva was quite agreeable to helping if it worked out.

Mrs. Justesen was in the attic when Ginnie came in from school the next day. With mop, pail, and vacuum cleaner, she had already imparted the special aroma of cleanliness she always left behind. "I hear you're going to have a day nursery!" she greeted Ginnie cheerfully, mopping away.

"I'm going to try and have one," Ginnie said modestly. "I have to find all the old toys I've got around and arrange them here. The horse can go over here." She dragged him into place. "Then the table and chair here. Would you help me bring up my doll carriage?"

The spirit of the undertaking seemed to communicate itself to Mrs. Justesen. She followed Ginnie to her room, and together they lifted the carriage up the steep stairs.

"Now I'll get my dolls," Ginnie began.

"If you want anything left of them, I wouldn't," Mrs. Justesen admonished.

"Well, I've got a great big rag doll. She'll be safe. Now I wonder where my old blocks are and my little tin dishes. And I'll bring up my baby books."

Mother unearthed the blocks and dishes in a box in the basement. "Here's a coloring book, only half used, and a box of crayons," Ginnie said, peering at the contents of the box. "I wonder where my old doll's bed is?"

"I'll look for it," Mother said. "And maybe I can get you a crate to use for a dish cupboard."

Mother and Mrs. Justesen were as interested in the playhouse project as Ginnie by this time. "Let me wash these windows," Mrs. Justesen said. "I'll get some fresh water."

"I could run up some curtains," Mother offered.

By five o'clock they had done all it was possible to do now. Mrs. Justesen departed, saying, "I never did wash the woodwork in the kitchen, Mrs. Fellows, but it'll keep till next week. First things first, and the attic's first today, seems like."

Ginnie conducted her father upstairs after dinner. He looked about, giving appropriate signs of approval. "It's all right. Operation attic. You go into business and I'll retire."

"I'll support you." Ginnie was supremely happy.

Next day she said to Geneva, "You have to come and see it! It looks just wonderful up there, with all the toys. Mother has some red material she's going to make curtains of. And she's going to get a crate for a cupboard."

"Where are you going to get the *kids?*"

"I'm going to see Mrs. Fraser and ask her if she won't . . . well, go out oftener or something." They both laughed.

Mother was in the attic when Ginnie ran upstairs after school. The gay red curtains hung at the windows. True to her word, Mother had contrived a cupboard out of a crate. The little dishes were displayed inside, and the opening was covered with a curtain that matched those at the window.

"Oh, it looks darling!" Ginnie breathed.

"And look what I found! Your old doll bed!"

Ginnie stood looking down at the little brass bedstead. It seemed a long time since she had seen it, and still not really long at all, it was so familiar. She looked up at her Mother, happiness shining in her face. "Oh, I just love this bed. Now everything's perfect!"

Then she followed Mother downstairs and pulled on a jacket. "I'm going to see Mrs. Fraser."

This time Susan came to Ginnie, snuggling into the big chair beside her. "She likes you," Mrs. Fraser said.

"And I love her!" Ginnie circled the child with her arm. "Oh, Mrs. Fraser, I want to tell you how I fixed up our attic! I've got toys up there—a rocking horse and a doll's bed and my carriage and blocks and everything. So when children come to be baby-sat it won't bother my mother at all, and they'll have just a wonderful time playing. And oh, Mrs. Fraser," Ginnie cried, "don't you want to go some place?"

Mrs. Fraser was a friendly and sympathetic young woman with a sense of humor, and she and Ginnie laughed together at the urgent appeal.

"I can see I'll have to go somewhere," she said. She thought for a moment. "I wish you were free earlier in the afternoon. I'd love to attend the League of Women Voters' afternoon discussion group, but that's from one-thirty to three."

"Couldn't they have it from three-thirty to five?"

"No, because mothers who have children in school want to get home before their children do."

Ginnie considered. "Could they start another discussion group? For ladies like you? Then you could all bring your children to my house."

Mrs. Fraser blinked a bit at that proposal. "You speak to the president," she said. "I can think of half a dozen women who would like to get to those meetings. But what would your mother say, for goodness sake?"

"Oh, she'll say it's fine," Ginnie assured her hastily. "Who is the president?"

"Mrs. Carteret. Do you know her?"

"My mother does. My mother goes to an evening discussion group. I'll ask her. . . ." Then she remembered that Mother had put the project strictly in her hands. "I'd better go see her," she said, with just a suggestion of a sigh, and withdrew her arm from Susan to get up. "Do you know her address?"

It was not as easy to call unannounced on strange Mrs. Carteret as it was to dash into Mrs. Fraser's friendly house. An almost outgrown shyness slowed Ginnie' steps. But if she was going to have children for her attic nursery . . . She set her jaw, forced herself up the walk, and firmly pressed the bell. Her heart was pounding. She almost hoped Mrs. Carteret was out.

Mrs. Carteret was at home. She was older than Mrs. Fraser. She had hazel eyes that looked kind, Ginnie thought. "Mrs. Carteret," she began, "my name is Ginnie Fellows."

"Oh yes," Mrs. Carteret said. "I know your mother very well. Will you come in, dear?" That made it easier. "What can I do for you?" Mrs. Carteret inquired.

"Well, you see . . ." Ginnie began. It was a long story, and she had not rehearsed it. "I want to earn some money, so I decided to do some baby-sitting. Only, well, I'm eleven, and most people want teenagers. So a couple of mothers have let their children come to my house. Only they, well . . ."

"Why don't you sit down?" Mrs. Carteret said kindly, indicating a comfortable chair and sitting down opposite.

Ginnie perched on the edge. "Anyhow, my mother let me fix up our attic. You know, with my old toys. So it's just like a nursery. And I was talking to Mrs. Fraser, and she said you were the president of the League of Women Voters."

Mrs. Carteret jumped at the sudden linking of her League and Ginnie's attic. "Why, yes, I am."

"And Mrs. Fraser — she lets Susan come over sometimes — Mrs. Fraser said maybe you would start a discussion group from three-thirty to five, for ladies who have little children who aren't in school yet. And the children could all come to my house and play in the attic. And I only charge fifty cents an hour instead of seventy-five!" She finished with emphasis, hopeful eyes on the League's president.

And Mrs. Carteret did not disappoint her. "Why, Ginnie!" she said, and she looked impressed. "You have really got an idea!"

Hope leaped up. Ginnie waited.

"Let's see." Mrs. Carteret thought. "There's Mrs. Fraser and Helen Duncan and Betty Moore and Barbara Cosgrove. Oh, and Ruth Levine and Mary Lou Abbott. But their little ones are too small. You couldn't manage babies who aren't walking."

"Yes, I can!" Ginnie cried. The solution was kind enough to present itself. "If they could bring playpens, I could have them in my bedroom. And I could get my friend Geneva to help!"

Mrs. Carteret was gazing at her with interest. "You're quite a girl. Here, have a peppermint." She passed the dish. "Now let me see. Our present afternoon group meets the second Thursday of the month," the League president went on. "If we could schedule one later the same day . . . Ginnie, give me your phone number. Let me talk to these girls and I'll call you. If we're going to do this thing, we might as well do it right away and have a meeting this month." She stood up, signifying the interview was over.

Ginnie got up too, thrilled and no longer ill at ease.

Mrs. Carteret wrote down the telephone number. "I assume your mother is agreeable?"

"Oh yes," Ginnie assured her quickly. "She helped me fix the attic all up. And she'll be home in case, well . . ." She trailed off, not wanting to say, "In case anything happens."

"Just in case. That's a good idea," Mrs. Carteret said with a smile.

Ginnie walked on air going home. She was not prepared for a setback when, at dinnertime, she reported to Mother the project that now loomed in the offing.

"But, Ginnie!" Mother protested. "Those girls have about eight children among them! For goodness sake, child, what are you getting yourself into?"

"You said I could!"

"I expected one or two at a time, not an attic full!"

"But it's only once a month. Other times I'd only have one or two!"

"What do you think, Ralph?" Mother asked.

"It sounds pretty advanced."

"Daddy . . ." Ginnie looked from one to the other, dismayed, not knowing what arguments to advance. Unexpectedly tears rose to her eyes. Which was a fortunate thing. Daddy could not bear to see his little girl cry.

"Well, you can always give it up if it doesn't work,"

he said hastily. "More steak?" Manlike, he considered food a cure for all troubles. Ginnie shook her head.

"But meanwhile, they'll have started the new discussion group," Mother said. "Well, they can stop it again, that's all. Maybe Grace Carteret won't round up enough women," she added hopefully.

But Grace Carteret rounded them up. Two nights later she called to say she had seven women interested — seven women with eight children. Two would come equipped with playpens. So, if it was all right with Ginnie, they would have their first meeting next week. The children would begin arriving about three-fifteen. The mothers would pay the rate she asked — fifty cents an hour.

Mrs. Carteret sounded brisk and matter-of-fact, as if she was quite unfamiliar with such a thing as failure. Her attitude bolstered Ginnie's courage, which had faltered a bit, faced with Mother's and Daddy's doubts.

But if eight small charges were arriving . . . It did rather take her breath. She must make sure Geneva could come and help her. She telephoned at once.

"They're going to do it, Geneva! What I told you — start that discussion group from three-thirty to five. And eight children are coming here next Thursday!"

"Wow!" said Geneva.

"So will you come and help me?"

"Sure!"

That night Ginnie had trouble getting to sleep. For the first time the magnitude of what she had blithely undertaken loomed large. She recalled, suddenly, the trouble she had had with Tommy when Susan insisted on his being Mrs. Bobbin. Suppose they all lay down on the attic floor and kicked and screamed? They wouldn't listen long to a story. And two babies in playpens in her room! Would Geneva be willing to stay with those two? That meant she would have six to handle herself. Mother might come . . . But no, Mother said it was all up to her.

The comforting thought came that, as Mother had said, they could stop the discussion group if things didn't work out. She wasn't taking on something she could not get out of.

But I don't want to get out of it! she thought. I want it to work. It's got to. She fell into a troubled sleep at last.

Nursery Day

THE ATTIC was ready for the onslaught tomorrow. Ginnie stood reviewing the plans which she had carefully made.

"Now, when they come," she said, talking out loud to keep her thoughts in order, "one of us can be downstairs. That ought to be Geneva. I'll be up here, so I can start them playing right off. The first one can play with Raggedy Ann in the carriage. If the second one's a girl, she can put Teddy to bed in the little bed. The next girl can play with the table and dishes. Then, for boys, I've got the blocks and that pounding toy and the coloring book. And when they've played for a while they can each have a cooky." She had a box in readiness. "Then I'll read them a story, and after that they can exchange toys and play some more!"

It sounded so easy. "The playpens can be in my room," Ginnie continued. "And Geneva can mind them, because that'll be easier than minding six little children."

She gave a final glance around and headed for the stairs. Now she must brace herself, and wait patiently.

She took up the plan with Geneva, walking to school. "You'd better take care of the babies in the playpens. That will be easier."

Unexpectedly, Geneva objected. "I want to be with the kids in the attic!"

"But we can't both be there. And I've had experience."

"How do you expect me to get experience if I have to sit and watch a playpen? I don't want to miss all the fun!"

"I think it would be fun to play with two darling babies," Ginnie said mildly.

"You play with them then."

"We'll take turns," Ginnie decided. "You stay with the babies for a while, and then I'll come down and you can go up."

School dragged interminably that day. Ginnie found herself looking at the clock repeatedly, and a mere ten minutes seemed to elapse when she was positive an hour must have passed. But three o'clock reluctantly arrived. Ginnie and Geneva began running the minute they were outside the building. They arrived at the house puffing as a car drew up and a small boy climbed out. His mother followed, carrying an even smaller girl.

"Hi!" Ginnie said.

"Hello. Are you Ginnie? Would you like to help me get this playpen out?"

The girls sprang to help her, and Geneva lugged the pen to the door. "I'm Mrs. Cosgrove," the mother said. "These are Peter and Penny. They've come to play and have a wonderful time. Haven't you, Peter?" Peter obliged with a nod.

They had established Penny in Ginnie's room and Ginnie was about to conduct Peter to the attic, when voices announced more arrivals. "You go down, Geneva," Ginnie said. "I'd better stay here." She and Peter stayed with young Penny, uncertain of her strange surroundings and inclined to be tearful, until Susan arrived. Susan, at least, felt at home now, although she appeared surprised and slightly resentful to find the room occupied by strangers.

Five to come. I'll get these two upstairs, Ginnie thought. She guided their steps up the steep flight. "Now! Susan, look what I have for you to play with!" She took the doll from the carriage. "And a little carriage to wheel her in. Won't that be fun?"

Susan gazed lovingly into Raggedy Ann's eyes, made maternal sounds, and kissed her soundly.

"And Peter," Ginnie went on, "you can play with these lovely blocks. You can sit right here on the floor."

"Ginnie, here's Karen!" Geneva called. Ginnie ran downstairs to escort a blonde, blue-eyed mite. "And Karen's little brother is here," Geneva added. "That's my quota."

Barbara Ann Duncan came, escorted up the stairs by her mother. Lucy Levine climbed bravely by herself. And lastly young Mark Abbott, obviously entertaining grave doubts about the whole thing, arrived on the scene.

Ginnie had no sooner introduced Mark to the coloring book than trouble arose in a far corner of this carefully laid out paradise. Small feminine voices arose, and Ginnie looked quickly to see Susan and Lucy in altercation over Raggedy Ann.

"Make a pretty picture, Mark," she said hurriedly. "Lucy, don't you want to put Teddy to bed in the darling little bed?" Lucy didn't. Lucy wanted to wheel Raggedy Ann in the darling little carriage. At least she did until Susan suddenly abandoned the big rag doll on the floor and commanded, "Dress up."

"Dress up!" echoed Lucy.

Oh dear, they can't all dress up, Ginnie thought. "Some other time, Susan," she said. "Now you play with these cute little dishes. You set the table. Lucy will help you." But Susan emphatically rejected Lucy's help. They're too little to play together, I guess, Ginnie thought, learning another lesson.

The boys were having trouble now. Peter had taken the coloring book away from Mark, and Ginnie avoided disaster by producing the pounding toy for Mark, which Peter instantly tried to appropriate also.

But she got them more or less organized at last. For a few blessed minutes harmony reigned in Ginnie's nursery, and then Mother called from downstairs, "Here's another customer, Ginnie. Tommy's mother decided to bring him too."

Tommy! Ginnie thought. Is he going to lie down and kick? But Tommy proved less of a problem than she feared, for Susan, looking up, instantly took charge. She trotted over to Tommy as he emerged from the stair well, reached out, and gave him two knocks on the head with her small fist.

"Oh," Ginnie said quickly, to forestall trouble, "Susan wants you to be Mrs. Bobbin, Tommy. Won't that be fun?"

Susan stood before her. "I be Mrs. Bobbin."

"Yes, you're Mrs. Bobbin too."

"Knock!" Susan shouted.

"Oh, yes!" Ginnie quickly knocked on Susan's forehead. Then Susan took Tommy's hand and escorted him to a corner of the attic. Perhaps it was shyness in a group of strangers or perhaps Tommy was resigned to co-operation with this determined female. But all was peace in Mrs. Bobbin's corner, as that lady's split personality went matter-of-factly through mysterious motions.

Peter pounded. Mark colored. Karen happily wheeled Teddy now. Lucy bustled about setting the table, and Barbara Ann sat serenely rocking a smiling Raggedy Ann.

It was going even better than she had hoped. I'll just run down for two seconds, Ginnie decided, and see how Geneva's getting on. Her ears had detected an ominous sound from below.

Geneva was sitting on the floor, dejectedly rolling a ball through the bars to small Penny, who gurgled as she laboriously squatted to pick it up and toss it with yelps of joy. But the small boy in the other pen scowled, tears on his round cheeks.

"What's the matter?" Ginnie asked.

Geneva shrugged. "He doesn't want to play."

Encouraged by a new audience, the unco-operative one opened his mouth and gave vent to heartbroken cries. "Oh!" Ginnie said. "Geneva, you go up with the others. They're all having a good time, so you don't need to do anything. I'll stay here."

Geneva needed no urging. She gave the ball a final toss, scrambled to her feet, and departed.

"Don't cry," Ginnie urged softly, and lifted the

grief-stricken small boy from his pen to walk up and down with him.

She had taken one turn when she heard the hubbub overhead. A shrill scream, a patter of feet, then Geneva's voice raised in admonition. Hastily Ginnie put the baby in his pen. "I'll be right back." She bestowed a hasty pat and flew for the attic stairs. "What happened?" she called.

"I don't know." Geneva stood there, looking baffled. Mark and Peter were looking up from their play. Barbara Ann seemed startled behind Raggedy Ann's fixed smile, and Karen and Lucy gazed with fascination at Susan. Susan, apparently taking a lesson from Tommy, had thrown herself on the floor and was sobbing as if her heart would break.

"What did you do, Geneva?" Ginnie cried.

"I didn't do anything!"

"Then what's she crying about?"

"I don't know. She and that little boy were sitting on the top step and I ran up and said, 'Hello, Susan, want me to play with you?' And she started to scream."

Ginnie bent over the anguished figure. "Come on, Susan. Ginnie's here."

Muffled sobs. "Mrs. B-Bobbin!"

Light dawned. "Oh! She isn't Susan, she's Mrs.

Bobbin; that's the trouble." She reached down and knocked twice, gently. The sobs subsided to small upheavals. "There now, Susan, get up. Ginnie is going downstairs for a few minutes, and Geneva will play with you."

But Geneva was off to a poor start. "Go with Ginnie," Susan said, one arm hiding her eyes. Ginnie stood still for a minute, torn between pleasure and perplexity. But all seemed quiet below, so she said, "I'll stay for a few minutes." Susan clutched her hand, wary eyes on that other big girl who had leaped up the stairs and insulted Mrs. Bobbin.

Geneva shrugged and turned to Tommy, who stood regarding the tempest with interest. "Well, then I'll play with you, Tommy."

Instantly Susan was dancing up and down, a small fury. "Mrs. Bobbin!"

"Oh, he's Mrs. Bobbin, too, Geneva! Susan, you knock, so he won't be Mrs. Bobbin." Susan subsided and released Tommy from thrall.

"Well, of all the . . ." Geneva said disgustedly, hands on hips.

"I can't help it," Ginnie said. "Now you can get Tommy busy."

"He can color," Geneva decided. "Mark can do something else. Here Mark, let Tommy have the coloring book." And Geneva unceremoniously removed book and crayon from Mark's fingers, producing a new uproar.

"Oh, Geneva, you have to give him something else! Here, Mark." Ginnie hastily wheeled the doll carriage over. "You wheel the carriage. Play it's a train."

But they had all been stirred up and could not settle back into peaceful play. No point in trying to read to them now, either, Ginnie decided. Susan was clinging to her as if she never intended to let go. She made a quick decision.

"I think we'll all have a cooky. And then we'll go outdoors," she announced. They could run there and let off the steam they had accumulated in almost an hour's sedentary play. She put cookies into outstretched hands. "Geneva, do you want to go down and put the babies' things on?"

"I suppose so." Though not a marked success with the attic set, Geneva still resented being relegated to the younger ones.

Ginnie herded the seven downstairs to the first floor, observing with an inward shudder that now seven small dusty hands braced themselves against the stair wall that Mrs. Justesen had recently made spotless. She helped her charges struggle into coats. Where was Mother? she wondered. Then she glanced out the window and saw her mother raking leaves.

"Let's go out the back door." They paraded through the kitchen and out the open door.

Ginnie ran to ask Mother to take charge for a minute or two, then hurried up to help Geneva get the babies and their pens down. At last they had them established in the yard. "Oh, I forgot the ball," Geneva said, and went in for one final trip.

Not only final, but fatal. Ginnie looked up as Geneva emerged, to see her pull the back door shut, and an awful premonition assailed her. The children were tearing about the yard now, releasing pent-up energies, and she walked to the back door and tried it. The door did not give.

She went over to Mother, standing, rake in hand, and watching the children. "Have you got a key, Mother?" she said.

"A key?"

"To the back door."

"Why no, the door's . . ." Mother turned to look at the door and uttered a small exclamation. "Who shut it?"

"Geneva. Maybe the front door's unlocked."

"Oh no, it isn't. And every downstairs window has a burglar lock!"

"What are we going to do?"

"Call the fire department, I suppose. I'll go over to Mrs. Ladd's and call."

Geneva had abandoned the two babies, who were both screeching now, and was trying to press the others into a game of tag. She had Karen by the hand, and they were pursuing a screaming Barbara Ann. The others followed Barbara Ann's example, running from Geneva with noise and determination. Susan, seeing Ginnie, fled to her for protection. In a minute Ginnie was mobbed by excited youngsters.

"They're too little to play like that, Geneva!" she called.

But Geneva, loving rough play, panting and glowing, did not heed her. "Come on, Tommy!" she shouted. "Let's tag one of the kids. Run, kids, we're coming after you!"

They clutched at Ginnie. "Stop, Geneva," she ordered finally. "It's too rough. I know, let's all play airplane."

This was play of an order they understood. "Let's start over here. Now we fly down the yard and see who can fly fastest."

The airplanes flew happily, flapping their wings. Ginnie flew with them while Geneva looked on, disapproving. Mother came back, and Ginnie called, "Fly back now," while she went to confer.

"They'll be here," Mother said.

The firemen were prompt. And from then on there was no need for organized play. Penny and Danny

looked on, big-eyed, leaning on the edge of their pens. The other children gathered in a fascinated group as two firemen brought a ladder. One of the men mounted it, pushed up a second-floor window, and disappeared inside.

It was just at that moment that the mothers arrived, to see a fire engine in front of the house where their precious ones were stowed for safekeeping. Mrs. Fraser led the race around the house, Mark's parent in close pursuit.

"What happened?" Mrs. Fraser called hysterically.

The others were there now, each snatching her child.

"It's all right. Nothing happened." Mother calmed them. "Somebody shut the door and locked us out, that's all."

Mothers with children clinging to them quieted down. They opened pocketbooks. "How did it go? Were they good?" Penny's mother asked.

"Oh — very good," Ginnie said quickly.

"Was Karen a good girl?"

"Was Barbara Ann?"

"Did you have a good time, honey?"

Children were sweet, Ginnie reflected, as each head nodded. They had had their little moments this afternoon, all of them, but already they had forgotten. They would come again, happily.

"Good-by, everybody!" she called, as mothers and children trooped around the house to the cars. "See you next month! And maybe sooner," she called hopefully for the mothers' ears.

They were gone at last, and silence descended, so noticeable it was almost uncomfortable. Ginnie turned back to the house as the last car drew away. "Well!" she said with a deep sigh. "It worked out all right." She decided quickly to ignore the locked-door episode.

But Geneva seemed in no mood to review the afternoon. "May I have my money, please, Ginnie? I have to go."

They sat down on the step. More than three dollars and a quarter apiece. "Isn't that better than making fudge or selling homely old Christmas cards?" Ginnie demanded happily.

"I suppose so. I'll see you tomorrow."

" 'By, Geneva."

Ginnie sat there, watching her friend disappear down the street. Geneva did not seem as elated as she was over their initial nursery session. Geneva was a little rough, and children had to get used to her.

And probably Geneva felt bad about locking the door. But she'll be all right when she has a little experience, Ginnie decided loyally.

Autumn Leaves

For the first time in days Ginnie's mind was at ease. The nursery was going to work out, she was sure. When Geneva called Friday night to suggest a hike on Saturday to see the foliage, Ginnie was delighted. She could relax now and really enjoy a day's outing.

"I'll ask if I can go," she said.

"Wait a minute." Ginnie could hear Geneva talking to someone. "Daddy says, does your father want to go too?"

"Daddy!" Ginnie called into the living room. "Would you like to go on a hike tomorrow with Geneva and her father? To see the autumn leaves? Oh, please go!"

"Fine!" Daddy called.

They set out on a perfect October day, a grape-blue haze soft over the landscape. Ginnie climbed happily into the back seat of the Porter car with Geneva. Mr. Porter stowed Daddy's knapsack in the luggage compartment with his own.

"Where are we going?" Geneva asked. Mr. Porter was the real hiker of the group. He had maps of trails for miles around, and had covered them all many times. Ginnie didn't care where they went. It was good just to be out of doors, heading for the woods and the hills this lovely lazy day.

"Shall we drive up to Pineville?" Geneva's father asked. "Near the reservoir there's an easy trail that climbs up over Mount Sharon. It shouldn't be too tough for you girls, and there ought to be some nice color."

"It can be as tough as it wants to be. We don't mind, do we, Ginnie?" Geneva retorted. Ginnie shook her head, smiling. She was agreeable to anything today, with not a worry in the world.

"I feel wonderful!" she said lazily, leaning back. "Especially, especially wonderful!"

"Why so especially?" Geneva demanded.

"Because the nursery turned out so well, I guess."

Geneva did not reply for a few moments. She gazed out the window, seemingly lost in thought as they sped along the highway past the outskirts of the town. "Some of those kids acted pretty awful," she remarked.

"Oh, they didn't really." Ginnie defended them quickly. "They were getting tired when you went up. You didn't know about Mrs. Bobbin, either," she remembered with a giggle.

"Mrs. Bobbin!" Geneva slid a withering look at Ginnie, and Ginnie laughed out loud. Geneva relented, giving a reluctant chuckle.

"Oh, Geneva, they're really cute!" Ginnie cried.

"I suppose so." Geneva was not convinced.

They dropped the subject then, to concentrate on the lovely autumn countryside. They were driving slowly along a winding road through woods glorious with autumn color, when Mr. Porter stopped at a turnout and consulted his map. "The trail should start right along here."

They came on the trail marker almost immediately. Mr. Porter parked the car by the road, the men shouldered their knapsacks, and Ginnie and Geneva ran ahead of their fathers, following the narrow trail that almost at once began to wind upward along a gentle slope.

Ginnie stood still suddenly. "What's the matter?" Geneva demanded, looking back at her.

"It's so quiet. You'd think we were miles and miles away." The quiet of the deep woods stretched out before her endlessly, it seemed. It's mysterious, Ginnie thought, not wanting to say it aloud lest Geneva think her queer. So many towns and people and cars on the road, and right here in the middle are these woods — all sort of secret.

She felt strangely moved and dropped back, waiting for her father. "Daddy?"

"Ginnie?"

Mr. Porter went on ahead, and Ginnie trudged along with her father. "Daddy, most people don't even know about this, do they?"

"Know about what, punkin?"

"These woods and this trail."

"I don't suppose they do."

"But how can it be here and everybody just drive by and never know about it? I should think millions of people would want to come here."

Daddy chuckled. "Aren't you glad they don't?" He glanced ahead to where Mr. Porter and Geneva were waiting. "Are we taking a breather?"

"A short one," Mr. Porter said. "We're about half-way to the top. Hungry?" he asked Geneva.

"Starved!"

"We'll eat when we get to the top."

Ginnie climbed silently after that, making her footsteps as quiet as she could. Now and then she started, as brush cracked near her. Once she saw the tail of a large rabbit that was leaping away. A squirrel scampered up a tree and chattered at them from behind the trunk. Along the trail there were glossy green bushes with scarlet berries, and sunlight struck deep down among the tall straight pines, turning the brown pine-needle floor of the forest to living russet.

Then Geneva was calling that she had reached

the top, and Ginnie ran to join her on an outcrop of rocks. They all stood together, looking out over a wide Persian-carpet expanse of woods and hills, stretching into the distance. One slim white village church steeple pointed to the sky.

Mr. Porter slipped out of his knapsack when they had drunk in the beautiful panoramic view. "Who wants a fire?"

"We do!" cried Geneva and Ginnie together.

"See what you can find in the way of firewood."

The girls gathered small twigs and branches. Ginnie's father brought back a good-sized cedar log. Mr. Porter carefully piled kindling in the center of the rock expanse, and Ginnie stood by, entranced, as the small wood fire crackled and the slender flames darted and danced.

Nothing had ever tasted as good as the hamburgers they cooked. There were potato chips, too, and tomatoes and pickles and toasted rolls. Ginnie munched in supreme contentment, sitting beside Geneva on the rock overlooking the view. It had been warm as they climbed, but now a shadow crept over the rock and she moved closer to the fragrant warmth of the bright fire.

"Did we bring marshmallows?" Geneva demanded.

"Certainly. What's a fire without marshmallows?" her father rebuked her, reaching into his pack.

After lunch they went on, down the other side of the slope and across a wooded valley. Deep in a dim-lit glade they crossed a cold rushing brook on pre-carious wet stones. But ahead in the sunlight the hill-sides paraded a pageant of many-shaded crimson and gold.

It was hard to turn back. But the sun was slant-ing across the pines now. Reluctantly they climbed back to their picnic spot, paused for one more long look at the world spread out below, and then Ginnie and Geneva sped down the path, which seemed so short going back, to the door out of the secret world of the woods. A car passed, and the occupants turned expressionless faces toward the two girls. They don't even dream how far, far away we've been, Ginnie thought.

Just the same, the car felt good after the long walk. The girls luxuriated in the comfort of the back seat. Ginnie felt her lungs replete with fresh air, her eyes still dazzled by the beauties spread before them. They were silent until Geneva sat up with an excla-mation.

Her father glanced over his shoulder. "Something wrong?"

"There was a dog."

"What about him?"

"He looked as if he was lost."

Mr. Porter slowed the car. "There aren't any houses around here."

"Please go back, Daddy!" Geneva cried.

Mr. Porter had brought the car to a stop now, and Ginnie looked back. "Here he comes!" she cried.

"I'm getting out to see him," Geneva announced.

"Take it easy with a strange dog," her father cautioned.

But Geneva was out, and a lean young collie was galloping toward her now, delighted to have found a friend. He capered about her, barking, his plumed tail wagging.

"Hello, boy." Geneva put out her hand. "Are you lost, you poor doggie?"

"Get into the car and see what he does," her father suggested. Geneva obeyed, and instantly the alert ears drooped. The brown eyes followed her, the tail slowed to a stop.

"Come on, boy!" Geneva said.

He was in the car, one happy, lively wiggle of a dog. He was on the seat, kissing Ginnie with his warm pink tongue. He was climbing onto Geneva's lap, lavishing love upon her until even Geneva shielded her face, laughing. "Get away! I don't want an elephant on my lap!"

They were all laughing now at the dog's joyous excitement. "He must be lost," Daddy said. "Why don't we take him to the nearest service station and see if they know him?"

Ginnie and Geneva rode several miles with the dog between them. At least they tried to keep him between them. He was all over the back seat, and breathed lovingly down the necks of the men in front. But Geneva was his favorite. He tried to climb onto her lap and lie down until Geneva was driven to discipline at last.

"That's enough!" she announced sternly, raising a finger. He paused, considering. "You lie down, sir," Geneva ordered.

Slowly, meekly, the lost dog obeyed, sitting on his haunches, tongue hanging out, and rolling his eyes toward Geneva to see if she really meant to be so stern. Ginnie and Geneva exchanged glances behind his back.

"You're good with dogs, Geneva," Ginnie said admiringly.

"I love them!" Geneva put her arm around the collie and laid her head against his side. His tail wagged in grateful homage.

They left him at the first service station they passed. Yes, the man said, he thought he did know where the dog belonged. "I'll give 'em a ring," he said. "He'll be all right here."

Geneva would not look back as they drove away. "I can't bear it," she said, her eyes tightly closed. "He wants to come with us. He thinks we're just going off and deserting him."

"You ought to have a dog, Geneva," Ginnie said.

"I wish I had a million dogs. But they make my mother sneeze."

Ginnie went back to school Monday, glowing in mind and body. But gradually, as the week passed, a slight concern over her nursery venture began to creep back. The first session had seemed successful, sure enough. But had it been, really? There had been the altercation between Geneva and Susan. Would Susan forget? And that scare over the fire engine. Would the mothers think she was a careless baby-sitter to let such a thing happen? Would they really bring their children back to her the third week in November?

She sighed, walking home from school after parting from Geneva. The third week in November was more than three weeks off. I hope I get to baby-sit with somebody before then, Ginnie thought. I hope Susan's mother has to go some place.

Wednesday morning Mother said, "Ginnie, you have to have a pair of shoes. I'll pick you up at school and we'll go downtown."

Ginnie brightened. A new pair of shoes was something to look forward to.

But when she stopped for Geneva the next morning, she learned what the new shoes had cost her. "Hey, guess what!" Geneva greeted her. "I sat with Susan yesterday!"

Ginnie stared at her blankly. "You — did?"

"Yes. Maybe her mother tried to get you first, I don't know. She had a toothache — Mrs. Fraser did. So she brought Susan to my house while she went to the dentist."

"I was out," Ginnie said bleakly. "I got these new shoes." The gleaming shoes dulled suddenly as she gazed down at them. She wanted to ask how Geneva had got along with her pet, but she was almost afraid to. Suppose Susan liked Geneva as well as she liked Ginnie? Suppose she liked her better!

She got it out finally. "Was she good?"

"No," Geneva said cheerfully. "She yelled. Finally I played the piano, and she liked that."

Ginnie felt her breath come more freely. She

sighed, a careful sigh of relief, which she hoped Geneva did not notice. It seemed that Susan was still hers. Her spirits began to rise.

And that very afternoon when she got home there was a message from Mrs. Fraser. Would she come and get Susan? Mrs. Fraser was going to have the tooth out.

Ginnie skipped over. Susan was waiting and Mrs. Fraser had her car keys in her hand. "She's been looking forward to it," Susan's mother said. "Did Geneva tell you she had Susan there yesterday when I couldn't get you?"

Ginnie nodded.

"Did she tell you Susan screamed all afternoon for Ginnie?"

"No." Ginnie's eyes widened.

"She did. You should be flattered."

Ginnie had rarely been happier than she was walking home with Susan's confiding hand in hers. They had a merry afternoon together. Ginnie knocked Mrs. Bobbin into being, and Mrs. Bobbin spent a busy day at her household chores in the attic. When Mother called upstairs to say Susan's mother was there, it did not seem possible that so much time had passed.

"Oh, Mrs. Bobbin," Ginnie said sadly, "good-by

for now." She reached out to give the required knocks on Susan's brow. "Oh, hello, Susan!" she cried delightedly. "Did you know your mother was here?" They tramped downstairs hand in hand.

"Do you know I've got to go back to that dentist tomorrow?" Mrs. Fraser said. "And it's Halloween. Susan has a costume, and she's been talking about Halloween for days, though she doesn't know what she's talking about. Would you like to take her out for a while?"

"I'd love to!" Ginnie cried. What bliss, to have Susan again tomorrow.

"My appointment is for five, of all ridiculous hours. Come over about a quarter of five, and I'll have her ready. Just go to a few houses."

"Just to people I know," Ginnie assured her.

"She's going to be a tramp." Mrs. Fraser went down the walk. "One tramp, small size, it says on the box the costume came in," she called, laughing, over her shoulder.

Ginnie considered getting into a costume herself. She loved Halloween, although she was a bit old now for dressing up. Maybe I'll ask Geneva if she wants to get a costume and come with us, she thought. But on reflection, she decided to say nothing. Why rub it in that Mrs. Fraser and Susan both seemed to prefer Ginnie as a sitter?

Geneva herself brought up the subject of Halloween, a bit wistfully. "Do you think we ought to go out on trick or treat?" she asked. "Of course it's mostly for little kids."

Ginnie hesitated. I'll have to tell her, she thought. "I'm going to take Susan out around five," she admitted. "I might put on an old dress or something. Want to come with us? Susan's going to be 'one tramp, small size.' "

"Oh." Geneva seemed a bit taken aback. "I guess not. Maybe I'll see if Lucy wants to go out with me later."

Ginnie knew that if she had been Geneva, she would have jumped at the chance to see Susan disguised as one tramp, small size. The thought suddenly occurred to her, I wonder if Geneva really likes children.

And just as suddenly a new worry loomed. Geneva had not made out too well with the children that first day. She had not been able to cope with Susan alone. Suppose the children wouldn't stay with her next time? Or suppose Geneva decided she didn't care for baby-sitting, especially on a large scale?

But I need her, Ginnie thought worriedly. I couldn't possibly manage seven children and two babies alone!

A Job for Geneva

As the time approached for the November meeting of the preschool mothers' discussion group of the League of Women Voters, Ginnie's anxiety grew, in spite of her self-assurances. Would the children really come again? Should she remind the mothers that she was still in business?

One passing worry, at least, had proved groundless. Geneva appeared to have every intention of staying with the nursery. She spoke of it several times. "When is it again?" she inquired one day on the way to school.

"It's next Thursday."

Geneva shook her head. "I certainly hope Susan doesn't yell all afternoon."

"She won't." Ginnie was not worried about Susan now.

She finally decided to make sure the children were really coming. She made a casual call on Susan's mother, using the excuse that she happened to be going by. "I hope you haven't had any more toothaches, Mrs. Fraser."

"No, thank goodness."

"I haven't seen Susan for quite a while."

"We've been busy."

"But I'll see her Thursday," Ginnie said.

"Thursday's the day," Susan's mother agreed.

That was a relief. Still, she briefly visited the entire group of mothers, to make sure there were no dropouts. Apparently all the children were to arrive as planned. Ginnie skipped home, a load off her mind.

She invested part of her profits in more blocks and another coloring book and showed them to Geneva.

"They're swell," Geneva approved. "Look, I still have some of my old toys. Want me to bring them over?"

"Yes!"

Geneva arrived at the house next day, wheeling a doll carriage filled with miniature dishes, pots and pans, and other remainders from her extreme youth. She chuckled, working the carriage through the front

door. "People must think I'm cuckoo, pushing a little
kid's carriage along at my age."

"I'll help you get it upstairs," Ginnie said. Geneva
really was nice, she thought warmly. She was a good
best friend. And she really wanted to help with the
nursery.

They were both pleased at the assortment of new
toys waiting to greet their charges. "We've got plenty
of things now," Ginnie said contentedly. "They won't
have to fight over who plays with what. Only they

probably will anyhow," she added philosophically.

"Ginnie," Geneva said, "let me be up here first, and you stay with the babies. I'll get them playing hide-and-seek, and then when they get tired you come up and read a story. And after that they can play with the toys."

Ginnie hesitated. "Geneva . . ."

"That's fair!" Geneva cried. "I stayed down in your room for ages last time!"

"All right." Ginnie wanted to be fair, of course. "But you have to be — kind of — well, quiet with them."

"Oh, I know," Geneva said carelessly. "Oh, Ginnie," she cried, as a new idea struck her, "I could bring my portable over and some records, and we could play musical chairs!"

"No! It isn't a party!" Ginnie cried. "They'll get all worked up."

"Oh, all right. Don't get excited."

Ginnie hoped for the best. Geneva seemed unable to grasp the fact that her tomboy ways were rough and startling for little children. She slept restlessly the night before the nursery session. In her half-waking moments she seemed to be forever cautioning, "Geneva, don't be so rough!"

Thursday morning, to Ginnie's surprise, Geneva

was not in school. "Can she be sick?" she wondered. It was dreadful, but she felt a faint stirring that might just be relief. If Geneva was sick — just a cold or something, of course — she wouldn't be able to come this afternoon. Then there would be no worry about the children's getting overexcited.

But if she doesn't come, Ginnie wondered then in sudden alarm, what will I do? Geneva might not be the most competent nursery assisant, but she had to have someone to help her. I'd better go around to her house this noon, she thought.

Then, for some obscure reason, she decided not to. I'll see if she comes to school this afternoon. If she doesn't . . . maybe I could get Anna! she thought suddenly.

Anna, who lived with Ginnie's grandmother, would be good at the job. She loved little children, and she was gentle and quiet and extremely competent for her age, Mother said. She'd like to do it, too, Ginnie decided.

She went straight home from school at noon, finished her lunch quickly, and hurried back. It was a temptation to go around by Geneva's house. Geneva would certainly expect her to come by and inquire. But, if she really was sick, surely her mother would have phoned to say she couldn't come this afternoon. It was puzzling. Perhaps Geneva did expect to be there, even if she had some reason for not going to school.

To be on the safe side she spoke to Anna. "I don't know where Geneva is, and this is our nursery day. Could you come and help me?"

"I'd love to!" Anna cried.

"Of course Geneva may come," Ginnie said. "But you come anyway." She couldn't invite Anna to help her and then at the last minute say she didn't need her.

Geneva was not in school for the afternoon session. She did not show up at Ginnie's, and there was no word from her. But with Anna on the job, everything ran smoothly. Anna kept the two babies drooling with happiness. She and Ginnie changed places, and after a brief explanation about Mrs. Bobbin, Anna took charge without seeming to take charge at all. Ginnie, below, kept one ear cocked, but all was peaceful in attic heaven. All the small charges were behaving like angels.

Anna led them down, smiling and willing, when the time came to go home. Today the children seemed relaxed and docile as they played in the yard. No firemen needed to be called. The mothers arrived and collected their offspring without incident.

"Did it go better this time?" Mother asked, when Anna had gone home.

"Yes. Anna's just wonderful."

"Better than Geneva?"

She felt disloyal. "She's had more experience. But it's the funniest thing that Geneva didn't come!"

Ginnie was so curious that she hurried around by Geneva's house in the morning. Geneva opened the door as she turned in at the walk. "Hi! Be right out."

She didn't sound sick. Ginnie was mystified. "Miss me yesterday?" Geneva called gaily, coming to join her.

"Yes, I did."

"Know where I went? I went to see some people my mother knows off on a ship for Europe. My mother said I could miss one day of school. It was exciting! Ginnie, that ship was as big . . ."

Ginnie listened in silence to a full account of Geneva's thrilling day. When Geneva had quite finished, she said, "I think you might have told me you weren't coming."

"I didn't know I was going till the night before."

"You could have called up."

Geneva looked at her in surprise. "Why do I have to tell you if I'm not going to school?"

"Not school," Ginnie said. "The nursery."

"But that's next Thursday."

"It was yesterday."

Geneva stopped short on the sidewalk, disbelief in her eyes. "It wasn't."

"It was!"

And then chagrin, disappointment, and embarrassment overwhelmed Geneva. She stamped her foot. "I — thought — it — was — next week! What did you do?"

"Anna helped me. She's *very good* with children," Ginnie said pointedly.

"Then that's all right." Geneva was recovering already. "I'll never forget again, I *promise!* I'll write it down on the calendar in great big red letters. I'll be there next time *or else!*"

"I was thinking," Ginnie said, trying to sound casual. "We might ask Anna to help us every time."

"No! That would cut our profits. Oh dear, and I was counting on that money!" Geneva knocked herself on the head. "Dope!"

"Mrs. Bobbin," Ginnie said, amused in spite of herself, and they both laughed as they quickened their steps to school. Ginnie did not pursue the subject. It was clear that Geneva considered she had a vested right in the project and did not intend to withdraw.

The lovely autumn color was fading into the drabness of early winter. The limbs of the maples stood stark and silent now against a colorless sky, and that afternoon a cold rain began to fall. Mother picked Ginnie up at school.

Something simmering on the stove filled the warm house with its meaty fragrance when Ginnie stepped through the doorway. "Vegetable soup," Mother said. "Oh, I meant to get some barley."

"I'll go," Ginnie offered.

"No rush. Are you hungry? I made some oatmeal cookies."

Early dark was falling when Ginnie donned raincoat and scarf, put Honey on his leash, and started for the store, head bent against the cold rain. They were halfway up the block when they met Mrs. DeGraw and Zabriskie. Mrs. DeGraw held an umbrella over her head and waited patiently while Briskie sniffed a tree.

"Hello, Mrs. DeGraw," Ginnie said. She paused to let the two dogs exchange greetings. "It's not a very nice day for you to be walking your dog."

"It isn't, is it?" Mrs. DeGraw agreed. "If I just had a girl like you I wouldn't have to take my poor old bones out in all weather."

"I like the rain," Ginnie said. "Honey and I both like it."

As she went along, it was Mrs. DeGraw walking Zabriskie that led Ginnie to think of the lost dog they had picked up the day of the hike. Hadn't he been glad to see them! And hadn't he liked Geneva! Geneva really loved dogs and knew how to handle them even though she had never owned one. She handles dogs better than she handles children, Ginnie thought. She . . . Suddenly Ginnie stood still as an idea struck her.

Geneva loved dogs. She would surely love to walk a dog if she had the chance. Mrs. DeGraw was old, and certainly could not enjoy taking Briskie out on such a day as this. So why couldn't that be a job for Geneva? If Mrs. DeGraw would pay her.

"I'll bet she would!" Ginnie said aloud.

Then — the logical sequel to her idea followed — if Geneva could earn some money walking the dog, perhaps she wouldn't care about helping with the nursery. If Geneva would withdraw, without Ginnie's asking her to, Anna would help gladly. Anna was wonderful with the children. She could be depended on. Everything would be fine. Ginnie's heart suddenly began to beat with high hope as she responded to Honey's tug on the leash and went on her way.

Next morning she hurried to Geneva's. "Geneva,

I had a wonderful idea! You said you needed to earn some money — specially when you missed the nursery. Well, yesterday I was going to the store when it was raining, and I met Mrs. DeGraw and Zabriskie. And I said it was too bad she had to go out in the rain with him, and she said, yes, if she just had a girl she wouldn't have to. So, Geneva, I'll bet if you ask her she'll let you dog-sit. I mean dog-walk! And pay you, I mean!"

Geneva seemed impressed. "Do you think she would?"

"Why don't you go and ask her?"

Geneva needed no convincing. "I'm going this very day."

Ginnie was in the attic that afternoon, helping Mrs. Justesen dust and clean, when a commotion downstairs sent her to the top of the steps. She could hear Geneva's voice, talking excitedly to Mother.

"Ginnie!" Geneva called.

"I'm here. Come on up."

There was a scramble below, and then Geneva appeared on the lower stairs. "Come on!" Geneva cried, looking behind her. And there was Zabriskie. Ginnie gave a small exclamation under her breath.

"Look who I've got!" Geneva shouted. "I'm going to walk him every day. And — careful, boy," she warned, as the big dog tried to squeeze past her on the narrow attic steps. " — she's going to pay me a dollar a week!" Geneva arrived puffing at the top of the stairs.

Briskie was all over the place — panting, sniffing, exploring. "Get along with you!" Mrs. Justesen cried, waving an indignant arm. "Shoo! Take him out of here, Geneva, I just got the place clean."

"Come on, boy." Geneva stood poised at the top of the stairs, but the boxer was too interested to obey. "Come on, Briskie."

"Here," Ginnie said, reaching for the box of cookies. "Show him a cooky and he'll go."

Geneva led the eager, sniffing animal back down the stairs. She was almost at the second floor when she called over her shoulder, "By the way, Ginnie, you'd better not count on me for the nursery in December. Do you mind? Because I have to walk Briskie every day now, and I don't think I can do both."

Standing at the top and gazing down on the pair descending pell-mell, Ginnie drew a breath, long, deep, and relieved. "Oh, I don't mind, Geneva," she said carefully. "I don't mind at all really. That's perfectly all right!"

Christmas Party

THANKSGIVING was a day of pale sunlight and delicious aromas stealing through all the rooms. Ginnie had helped Mother stuff the turkey the night before. She crumbled the bread in a pan, shook in poultry seasoning, and poured melted butter. She had to taste it frequently. "This is good. Why don't we have it sometimes without turkey?" she inquired, scooping up another bit. She spooned and packed until the big bird bulged.

At eleven o'clock they were in the crowded church for the Thanksgiving service. I'm thankful, Ginnie thought, sitting between Mother and Daddy. I'm thankful that the nursery is working out and that Geneva has a dog to walk.

Grandma and Anna joined them after church, and they all went home to help in the kitchen. Even

Daddy wandered in briefly, drawn by the tantalizing odors, while Honey lay in the middle of the floor, on hand for any and all delicious tidbits. Daddy finally led him out, sad and reluctant, for a holiday stroll.

"Anna," Ginnie said, when dinner was over and the kitchen cleared of signs of the holiday feast, "come on up in the attic and see if you've got any good ideas for the nursery."

They were up there, sitting in two small chairs and discussing ways of keeping small children happily occupied, when Ginnie said, cocking an ear, "I think I heard the doorbell."

There were voices. In a minute Geneva was calling up the stairs, "Hi, kids!"

"Hi! Come on up," Ginnie called back.

Then she realized, from the scuffling below, that Geneva had Briskie with her. A moment later she wondered if she were seeing double. Geneva had two dogs.

"I'm walking Snuffy too," Geneva announced, out of breath. "I thought of Miss Wilson — you know, the lady who lives next door to us — so I asked her if she wanted me to walk her dog too, and she did, sometimes. Careful, boys." The animals were pushing eagerly ahead. "Calm down, boys!" Geneva commanded.

The dogs were clambering over Ginnie. She patted their heads, but Briskie, especially, seemed unusually persistent.

"It's the cookies," Geneva said. "You gave Briskie some, remember? That's why he was so crazy to get up here."

"Oh. Well, I've still got some." Ginnie went to the box, and the dogs practically mobbed her, barking vociferously.

"You animals!" She fended them off. "Here, eat your cookies and behave yourselves." She held out a cooky in each hand, and the warm eager mouths had them in a twinkling.

"Now down!" Geneva instructed. The dogs finally obeyed, licking their chops and keeping their eyes on Ginnie, the giver of cookies.

Geneva sat on the top step and the girls visited, until Geneva said, "I suppose I'd better finish walking them. Aren't I lucky to have a job even on Thanksgiving?"

"You must be rich!" Anna remarked.

"I'm rolling," Geneva said placidly. "You kids want to go Christmas shopping some afternoon?"

"I'm not going to buy much," Anna said.

"I spent a lot for toys, so I haven't got too much money," Ginnie replied. "I'll have to do most of my Christmas shopping after the fifteenth." The December nursery date had been set a week early because of the holidays.

"I'll lend you some." Geneva could well afford to be magnanimous. But both Ginnie and Anna preferred to proceed on a cash basis.

"I might have some sitting to do with Susan, if Mrs. Fraser wants to go Christmas shopping," Ginnie said hopefully.

So it turned out. The next days brought several sessions with Susan. Ginnie and Susan were fast friends now. Ginnie's attic was a magic playroom to the child, and she headed straight for it when she came into the house. But before Susan could make use of the carriage, the little bed, the table and dishes, the Mrs. Bobbin rigmarole was essential. Ginnie automatically knocked Mrs. Bobbin into being. She herself could then retire to a chair beside the window and keep one eye on her charge while she read or did homework. Mrs. Bobbin was self-sufficient. She bustled about, conversing with unseen companions, laughed merrily in the course of long murmured phone conversations, and conducted her numerous duties in businesslike fashion.

Only occasionally interest waned. Then Susan would come over and lean against Ginnie's knee.

"Want a story now, Susan?"

Mrs. Bobbin gazed at her blankly. "Oh, excuse me, Mrs. Bobbin. I thought I was speaking to Susan!" Ginnie tapped Mrs. Bobbin's brow. "Now would you like a story, Susan?"

With a sigh of happiness Susan climbed into Ginnie's lap. Her small head, so shiny and clean-smelling, against Ginnie's shoulder, the little girl listened entranced. Ginnie enjoyed this part of her job most. She went through her books, picking out stories she knew Susan would enjoy.

Mrs. Fraser asked her one day what she knew about Mrs. Bobbin. "Susan keeps talking about her. She sounds like a very close friend."

Ginnie giggled. "She is. She's Susan. I mean Susan is Mrs. Bobbin. She plays Mrs. Bobbin all the time."

"Mrs. Bobbin likes frankfurters, and Mrs. Bobbin has a green cat, and Mrs. Bobbin has a number of children — twenty-six, I believe," Mrs. Fraser informed her.

"That's why she's so busy," said Ginnie, highly amused.

"Do you have any trouble at all with Susan?" the child's mother asked curiously. "Does she have little temper tantrums?"

Ginnie shook her head, then remembered. "Oh,

she did once. But it's just if you forget about Mrs. Bobbin."

"You must have a way with children. You've certainly won Susan over," Mrs. Fraser said. Ginnie flushed a little with pleasure at the compliment.

December had come in, as December should, with a drop in the temperature and a sting in the gray air. Christmas lights were strung along Main Street, and Ginnie liked to walk Honey at dusk, so she could admire their red, blue, and green gaiety. Shop windows were rimmed with frost, tinsel trimmings winking within.

"Please come shopping with me!" Geneva begged one afternoon.

Ginnie had not done any shopping, and she longed to. She got out her pocketbook and counted. The nickels and dimes and quarters were heavy but did not add up to very much. She finally borrowed from her father. "I'll pay you back after the children are here."

"That's all right, punkin. I think you're entitled to some Christmas money."

"Oh, thank you, Daddy!" Ginnie threw her arms about his neck. "Now I've got heaps!"

But once she was launched on shopping, the money did not last long. Ginnie had set her heart on buying a present for each of her nursery children. She and Geneva visited the ten-cent store, and she found balls for the babies. But the labels on the other toys seemed depressingly expensive. Nine presents, even at a quarter apiece, added up. "Why do they call this a five-and-ten, anyhow!" she inquired disgustedly.

She went home laden with packages. But she had nothing yet for Mother, Daddy, and Grandma, or for Geneva and Anna. Wrappings and Christmas cards had taken a further bite.

But Ginnie was happy as she dumped her purchases on the kitchen table and proudly displayed them, one by one, to Mother and Daddy. She hummed to herself as she carried the armful of presents to her room and stowed them in the closet. She would wrap them soon, but meanwhile she wanted to take them out and look at them and to picture the children's excitement as she presented them. She would save them as a surprise for the end of the session.

And maybe we can have a little Christmas party, she thought. With cookies and apple juice. Oh, and maybe I can fix up a little tree . . .

It was such fun. She went to the cellar and rummaged in the box of Christmas tree ornaments to find the tiniest ones. She spent another dollar and ninety-eight cents out of her dwindling fund for a small tree, coated to look snowcovered. She rounded up enough chairs, stools, and boxes to seat them all.

Everything was ready when the day came — the gaily decked tree with presents piled around it, apple juice and small paper cups, and napkins rimmed with holly. Ginnie had made Christmas cookies shaped like stars, and a Christmas story was carefully selected.

The children trudged upstairs, eager and looking forward to the now-familiar playroom. There was a rush for the tree, which Anna defended. Anna could handle them, Ginnie thought, as she ran downstairs to take her turn with the babies. She would go up later for the story hour and party.

The babies were good. When the time came for her to go up, Ginnie waved to the playpen set and hurried upstairs. How she was looking forward to the fun!

"Now," she proclaimed gaily, arriving at the top, "we're going to have a story. And then we're going to have a party!" Party was a magic word. They dropped their toys and gathered round. Susan was deBobbinized. Ginnie read them a story that left stars shining in their eyes.

She closed the book slowly, smiling into their absorbed faces. "Now we're going to have presents. Then we'll have the party!"

Anna read names and handed out presents. Ginnie saw that each present stayed in the right hands. The floor was strewn with Christmas wrappings. Excitement ran high as little girls minutely examined the new treasures and small boys got down on the floor to try out miniature trucks and cars.

"ZZZZZzzzz!" buzzed Mark, flat on the floor, racing his army truck.

"MMMMMmmmm!" hummed Peter happily, his racer scooting about.

"They love their presents!" Ginnie murmured delightedly to Anna, watching the excitement.

They let the children play with their presents for a while. Then, as interest began to flag, Ginnie announced, "Put your presents on the bureau for just a few minutes. You can take them home later. We're all going to sit down and have the party. Let's put our chairs in a circle again."

They were businesslike, drawing up seats. They sat expectantly, while Ginnie poured apple juice and Anna passed cookies.

And so they were all engaged, mouths ringed,

hands crumby, but good as angels as they enjoyed their Christmas party — when disaster struck.

It struck in the form of a whirlwind coming up the stairs. "Geneva, keep those dogs down here!" Ginnie heard Mother call out. But to no avail. Ginnie stood frozen, pitcher in hand, as Geneva's two animals romped boisterously up the stairs into the midst of the happy circle.

"Hey, dogs, come here!" Geneva shouted, her head appearing.

She could not control them. The attic was full of the delicious smell of cookies clutched in small hands and cooky crumbs on the floor. Eager dog noses rooted into laps and faces, licking, kissing, lapping up crumbs.

Pandemonium broke loose. Karen's stool overturned, depositing Karen on the floor, prey to a dog's overpowering affection. As soon as Karen could get her breath she used it to utter piercing shrieks, fending off dogs with both hands. Peter, it seemed, liked dogs. He got his arms around Briskie, his face wet with kisses, before he, too, tumbled off his chair. Barbara Ann ran screaming to Anna. Susan edged back against the wall, holding a cooky high in the air. Lucy clutched Ginnie's skirt, shouting at the dogs, "Go 'way!" Mark pounded with his fists on whatever dog whisked near him, receiving smacking caresses in return.

Over it all Geneva was shouting, "Down, boys! Briskie! Snuffy! Come here! Lie down, sir!" to which, this time, her two charges paid no heed whatsoever. They were having a Christmas party. Anna snatched the plate of remaining cookies and held it high, to save it from the dogs.

And the mothers arrived. Normally the children were outdoors. Today time was forgotten in the scuffle, dogs and children all worked to a feverish pitch of excitement. Guided by shrieks, the bang of overturned stools, the mothers one and all hastened to the rescue.

Children rushed screaming to safety. Geneva got her hands on the dogs at last and forcibly calmed them. Ginnie stood stricken, not knowing how to apologize or explain.

"It wasn't . . ." she began. But how could she say, "It wasn't our fault; it was Geneva's"? There was really nothing to do but begin to pick up the overturned stools while she thought about what to say.

Geneva had the grace to apologize. "I shouldn't have let them come up. But I didn't know you were having cookies and everything! And they wouldn't hurt the children, they love them!" She patted Briskie's head as the two beasts lay panting and still eager-eyed beside her.

The mothers were sensible young women, and once their initial alarm was quieted they wiped their children's tears away and exclaimed over the presents exhibited for their admiration. One by one, restored to calm, the children were led downstairs, chattering happily now of the gala events of the afternoon.

Ginnie followed soberly. "You stay here till they've gone, Geneva," she said severely. "I don't want those dogs to get mixed up with the children again."

Geneva was properly meek.

In Ginnie's room the two babies were echoing the shrieks above stairs. Their mothers gathered them up.

Ginnie stood on the second floor, gazing down. She should go down, she knew, and help gather coats and say good-by. But she wanted to go into her room and fling herself on the bed and cry at the horrible, unexpected ending of her so lovingly planned Christmas party.

"Don't feel bad, Ginnie." It was Anna, beside her. "It wasn't your fault."

The kind words were too much. Tears welled into Ginnie's eyes. She could not face those mothers below. They would never, never let their children come here again, to be frightened to death by dogs. And it *was* her fault. She was in charge, and she had permitted it to happen. Ginnie turned blindly, rushed into her room, and shut the door behind her.

End of a Dream

GINNIE SAT DISCONSOLATELY in the big chair at the living-room window. She was staring out, but she saw nothing of the dull December landscape. Instead, she saw the collapse of her hopes.

Mother had said little last night about the afternoon's fiasco. Ginnie had been so crushed then that she could not have discussed it. But this afternoon Mother had brought up the subject over the three-o'clock snack.

"It isn't good for you to be so absorbed in this project, when — really, you know — it's a little beyond an eleven-year-old girl."

"It isn't beyond me! Everything was fine, until Geneva . . ." She pressed her lips together.

Mother reached for Ginnie's emptied glass and carried it to the sink. "This discussion group for preschool mothers was an experiment, you know. I'm not sure they'll go on with it during the bad weather, anyway."

This was a blow, quite aside from yesterday's events, but Ginnie grasped at any straw. "Maybe I can get some other children."

Mother hesitated. "I noticed the attic was a bit on the chilly side yesterday. I don't believe you can use it during the winter. You may have Susan in your room, dear, but suppose we leave it at that."

Ginnie went wordlessly into the living room and threw herself into the chair. The world lay bleak about her. She loved Susan, of course, and she could have her here, at least, but her beloved nursery, so exciting, so fun-filled and satisfying, was a thing of the past. Why can't I be thirteen, she fumed, wriggling with frustration. Then I could go to people's houses and baby-sit. It's just terrible not to be old enough! I *am* old enough, she told herself. It's just mothers. They're stupid.

She got up finally and took her coat from the hall closet. "I'm going out for a while," she called.

She was going to see Mrs. Fraser. She had to know firsthand the reaction to yesterday's incident, and find out whether they really were going to end the discussion group, whether they were all mad at her, or what. Despite all Mother had said, she could not bear to give up.

Susan was having a nap. "She was so worked up after that business with the dogs, she had a restless night," her mother said.

"I'm very sorry it happened," Ginnie said soberly. "And it's never, never going to happen again." She gave Mrs. Fraser this opening and waited, holding her breath.

"Yes. Well," Mrs. Fraser said, "I don't believe we'll be having the discussion group again this winter. January and February are such bad months."

"Will you have it again in the spring?"

"We'll see when spring comes."

Mrs. Fraser gave no indication that yesterday's occurrence was involved in the decision to discontinue. Ginnie tried to tell herself that they would have stopped anyway. But that frantic excitement, she could not help knowing, had not furthered the cause of her nursery.

So that was that. She walked slowly home, let herself in, and slid out of her coat. Then, propelled by some inward urge, Ginnie quietly climbed the stairs and went on up to the attic. Mother had brushed up the crumbs and removed the remains of the party. The little tree stood deserted and dim. It was distinctly cold here, cold and damp. She hadn't noticed it at all yesterday. She walked about, touching the little horse, the doll bed, and the carriage. Then she went down. Her wonderful dream was at an end.

She thought of Geneva and the dogs. Geneva had been properly contrite today, and firm in her assurance that the miserable beasts would never again visit Ginnie's attic.

"You bet they won't," Ginnie had said grimly.

But the next morning Geneva seemed to feel that she had properly expiated her crime. She had put it aside and expected Ginnie to do likewise. Geneva was, in fact, inordinately cheerful. She had acquired a third dog to walk. It did not improve Ginnie's state of mind that Geneva, so inept at running a nursery, should be such a success in an undertaking that she herself had launched.

She did not tell Geneva that the nursery had had its last session. She merely said glumly, "Maybe I ought to walk dogs."

She did go out that afternoon with Geneva, to walk Briskie. It was something to do, something to take her mind off her own failure. Geneva chattered gaily. "Only one week to Christmas! Have you got all your shopping done?"

"No, have you?"

"No. I like to save some, so I'll be in a terrible rush. I adore being in a rush. It makes the time go faster." Peter was coming toward them with his bag of papers, whistling cheerfully. "Hi, Peter!" Geneva called.

"Hi."

"Done your Christmas shopping?" Geneva shouted.

"Nope."

But at least, Ginnie reflected, he had money to shop with from all those papers he collected for every Friday. Peter was saving his earnings to go to college, she knew, but he was never short of spending money. She seemed to be the only one who was out of funds. She had spent practically every cent she had on the Christmas party. Her proceeds from yesterday's session provided only meager means with which to set out on Christmas shopping for family and friends.

And after Christmas, Ginnie thought bitterly, Geneva would still have her dogs to walk, while she, Ginnie, would be right back where she started. She wasn't even sure she would have any baby-sitting with Susan, after that business with the dogs.

It was Daddy who came to the rescue again. When he gave her her allowance he said, "How about a little extra margin, to buy your mother a present?"

"You gave me some extra."

"I know, but I want to give you some more. It's the Christmas spirit. I want to be sure you get me something worthwhile."

"Oh, Daddy!" She couldn't quite laugh at her father's humor. "Thank you, anyhow." She was grateful if not exuberant.

He had another suggestion. "How about you and me going shopping some night? I think the stores are open late now."

"Just you and me?"

"I need your advice on something for your mother."

With this prospect in view Ginnie's spirits picked up. "Could we go shopping in New York?"

He looked dubious. "I had in mind just trying a couple of shops here."

"But I love New York at Christmas time!" Ginnie cried. "Can't we please, Daddy?"

So it was arranged. Mother put her on a bus at five o'clock, and Ginnie forgot her troubles at last in the excitement of traveling into New York by herself, having dinner with Daddy, and walking along Fifth Avenue, where the store windows were a yuletide fairyland.

Being in New York with Daddy was different from being here with Mother. Daddy took her to a manlike restaurant, where there were men waiters, and he ordered sirloin steak and French fried potatoes, with cherry-stone clams, which Ginnie greatly relished, first. As she happily dipped the clams into their spicy sauce and let them slip down her throat and nibbled crisp little salted crackers, Ginnie felt Christmas catch at her spirits at last. She looked around the humming, busy restaurant, and was happy.

Shopping with Daddy was different too. He made up his mind quickly and didn't even ask prices. They bought Mother an angora sweater in a shade of lilac so lovely Ginnie was in raptures. The thistle-down-soft wool seemed nothing in her hand.

"What can I get for her?" she asked.

They wandered about the main floor of the great store, so glamorous with its silver decorations and the sound of carols and wonderful smell. It was the fragrance that led Ginnie to the perfume department, and she found toilet water and matching bath powder that smelled so deliciously of lilies-of-the-valley that she made up her mind instantly.

When the package was put into her hands, it was gift wrapped in gold paper with a huge sapphire-blue bow. It was sheer delight to carry such a Christmas package. Ginnie turned from the counter, cheeks flushed with pleasure.

"Have we finished?" Daddy inquired.

"I guess so." She gazed about. "I'd like to spend the night here."

He laughed at her. "How about an ice-cream soda before we head for home? Or is it too cold?"

"No! It's not cold at all!"

The interlude in Schrafft's, filled with gay and thirsty shoppers and twinkling with Christmas decorations, helped to forestall the inevitable plunge out of the bright city into the dark suburbs. Ginnie decided on a hot fudge sundae with chocolate ice cream and pecans, and ate it as slowly as she could, savoring every mouthful.

"Some day," she informed her father, "I'm going to come to New York and spend a whole week at a hotel and do everything. When I'm rich," she added. That reminded her of certain unhappy events. "I mean *if* I'm ever rich," she said glumly.

Daddy patted her shoulder. "Nobody ever got ahead without a few setbacks. They tell me you're a whiz with the juniors. In a few years you'll have all the business you can handle."

"Who said I was a whiz?" Ginnie asked, surprised.

"Your mother mentioned it."

"Oh." She considered. "Well, she's prejudiced." But the compliment cheered her up. "Oh, well!" she said philosophically, and sought to dismiss the subject from her mind again.

From then on the days were filled to the brim with the rush of Christmas preparations. Mother made mincemeat. Ginnie helped her, chopping the suet, separating raisins and pieces of citron. The great black iron kettle, which had been Grandma's when Mother was a little girl, bubbled and simmered and filled the whole house with tantalizing spice. Ginnie kept ladling out small dishfuls of the hot fresh mincemeat to eat. The day before Christmas Mother would ladle the delicious, meaty mixture into jars, tie them with red bows, and give them away as presents.

There were other quick shopping expeditions with Mother after school. Mother's gift had almost exhausted Ginnie's Christmas fund, but after long searching she found a tie for her father in his favorite Scotch plaid and a box of especially pretty note paper for Grandma. She found books for Anna, Geneva, and Peter and a new rubber bone for Honey. Mumbo would find a can of mackerel under the tree, strong and fishy and the delicacy of all delicacies so far as a little black cat was concerned.

There was the usual thrill of Christmas Eve, with Grandma and Anna there to spend the night. Daddy brought in the tree, and Ginnie and Anna had it partly trimmed before supper. There was a fire in the fireplace, and they ate in the light of the leaping flames and the twinkling many-colored stars set among the balsam branches. The girls hung their stockings, plus one each for Honey and Mumbo, but lingered late by the fire. Ginnie hated to leave the warm, shadowed room, fragrant with evergreens, and the pile of mysterious packages beneath the tree. Christmas Eve is almost better than Christmas morning, she thought.

"It's bedtime for two somebodies," Mother said finally.

Ginnie stretched lazily, smiling sleepily at her. "Oh me!" She reached out her arms in a wide embrace of Christmas. "We'll take Geneva's presents over in the morning," she said. "And Peter's, too."

"Snow's predicted," Daddy remarked.

"Oh, I hope we have a white Christmas!" Anna cried out.

Despite the forecast of snow, Christmas Day dawned in sunshine to match the gaiety of Christmas spirits. There were the presents, and sausages for breakfast. Then the trip to Geneva's and Peter's and the happy exchange of gifts.

They had dinner, topped with warm, juicy mince pie. It was cold enough for skating, and both girls had found new skates under the tree, so after dinner Daddy walked with them to the pond, where a hoisted red ball proclaimed the ice safe.

And as they walked home in the dark, Christmas lights shining from every window, the first soft snowflakes began to fall, drifting in fragile, silky fragments across Ginnie's upturned face.

There were turkey sandwiches and cocoa for supper. "I thought I'd never be hungry again," Ginnie declared, "but I changed my mind."

"Me too," Anna echoed.

After supper they played new records that had come for Christmas, until at last Daddy said, looking at his watch, "Well, Christmas is over for another year. Come on, and we'll drive Grandma and Anna home."

Christmas was over. Ginnie's heart, which had put its troubles aside for a season, gave a sudden sick drop. What will I have to think about after Christmas, she asked herself, with no nursery or baby-sitting?

She drove home with Daddy through the snow-filled night. The ground was white now. "Looks as if it may be settling in for a real snowstorm," Daddy remarked.

"Good," Ginnie said. A snowstorm was something happening, at least.

Surprise

GINNIE AWOKE the morning after Christmas in the grip of an all-over dismal feeling. She lay blinking at the gray light as Mother came in. Mother pulled up the shade.

"Good morning, dear. Have you looked out?"

Ginnie rolled over and looked, then sat up with a gasp. The flakes of snow, so fine and melting last night, were mammoth furry things now, falling madly, endlessly. Pure snow drifted in peaks and swirls on the roofs, the trees stood coated in white, the untrod ground lay deeply covered.

"Oh, boy!" Ginnie gasped.

She put on her bathrobe and went down to a late breakfast, depression lost in a stir of excitement. Mother heated coffee and sat down with her.

"They predict a real blizzard," Mother said. "Daddy didn't even try to get the car out. He took the bus."

"I hope we do have a blizzard!" Ginnie cried.

"At least we've got cold turkey in the house," Mother commented.

"I adore cold turkey."

Ginnie wandered into the living room, plugged in the Christmas tree lights, and went through her pile of presents again. She read a few pages in the book Peter had given her, examined her new red-leather pocketbook, and tried on the new gloves. When she went up to dress she carried the book with her and flung herself down on the bed, lost in the story.

But at last she sat up and looked out the window. Winds, like small hurricanes, were spinning the snow in circles. I'm going out, she decided. The cold air and wet snow would feel fresh and good after the warm house. She put on slacks and a sweater and went downstairs.

"Is it all right if I go over to Geneva's?"

"If you don't get lost in a snowdrift."

"I'll stay to lunch if her mother invites me," Ginnie said.

Mrs. Porter invited her, but Mother called soon after to say it was snowing and blowing so hard that she had better come home.

The snow was almost up to her knees. Plows had come along the streets, throwing the snow into drifts at the crosswalks, and Ginnie plunged in up to her waist. She was soaked and panting, but glowing with cold and exertion as Mother opened the door. "Oh, I love it!" she gasped. "I could stay out forever!" But it felt good to get into dry clothes and snuggle into the big chair with her book.

Daddy got home late that night and reported that the snow had brought traffic virtually to a standstill. It was still snowing next morning when Ginnie looked out. All day the flakes fell furiously into a world already lost in whiteness. Daddy did not go to work. He and Ginnie played Scrabble cozily through the short, dim afternoon. Heavy snow was still tumbling endlessly down under the street light when she closed the book she had taken to bed with her and peeked out. She turned off her light and rolled up the shade, giving a delicious shiver as the warmth from the hot radiator rose between her and the storm raging beyond the snow-fringed window.

Some time in the early hours the falling flakes lost their purpose. On the third morning Ginnie awoke to a glassy world, dazzling under brilliant sunshine, the rainbow crust of the snow tossing off the colors of jewels.

After breakfast she and Daddy went out to shovel. "Two feet, at least," Daddy estimated.

"And look along the road!" Ginnie exclaimed. The drifts thrown up by the plows were higher than her head. The streets stood white, silent, and deserted.

She could make little impression with her shovel, although the snow was light. Even Daddy, trying to dig out the car, gave up. "It can stay here," he said, and they stamped the snow from their stinging feet and went in to eat pancakes for lunch.

But even snow excitement palled after a time. That afternoon Ginnie was restless, pacing from room to room. "What a Christmas vacation!" she grumbled, staring out the window. "Can't go anywhere. Nobody can come here!" Even the short walk to Geneva's house was out of the question, with sidewalks only partially shoveled.

Mother gazed over her shoulder. "I have a bee in my bonnet."

"What?"

"This might be a good time to have some people in to supper. I've been wanting to entertain the Frasers and the Olsens — and that young couple, the Sebrings, who just moved in down the street. They can't drive anywhere, but they might be able to get over here in a day or two."

Ginnie swung around joyfully. "Oh, let's! Oh, and if the Frasers come, can they bring Susan?"

"I suppose they'd have to. She could go to bed in your room."

"Could she stay all night?" Ginnie cried.

"She might not want to."

"She would with me," Ginnie said confidently.

Mother began planning. "I've got that ham and plenty of salad things, and we could have scalloped potatoes . . ."

"Can I make something?" The prospect of a party was a tonic for dullness.

"How about making a cake? Or some rolls?"

"Both," Ginnie decided.

Her enthusiasm helped spur the plans, and that evening Mother phoned the invitations to a buffet supper. "Well," she announced gaily, turning from the last telephone call, "everybody's delighted to come tomorrow night. They're all bored to death with staying home."

"Is Susan coming? Can she stay all night?"

"They're bringing her. Yes, if she doesn't object, she can sleep here, and her father will get her in the morning."

"Oh, good, good!" Ginnie spun around. "Can we start right now getting ready?"

"We'd better. There's plenty to do." Mother took a pad and pencil and sat down. "I think we'll have that jellied mold with apricots and cherries, it always looks so pretty. Why don't you make an angel-food cake? And we'll ice it with whipped cream and strawberries. There's a mix in the cupboard."

Ginnie was up early next morning. She never felt happier than when she was getting ready for a party, and all day she sang as she and Mother worked in the kitchen. The angel-food cake came lofty and golden from the oven. Ginnie helped add leaves to the dining table and lay the damask cloth, gleaming like satin. The Christmas centerpiece of greens and cones was still lovely, the slim scarlet tapers in the silver candlesticks scarcely burned.

In the late afternoon Ginnie's rolls rose, light and perfect, under a clean tea towel. The ham was pink and luscious, the tossed salad glistened under its dressing in a Chinese bowl, and the jellied mold was festive. At five o'clock Mother slid the casserole of potatoes into the oven. The cream was whipped for last-minute icing. Ginnie walked slowly around the dining-room table, admiring. She could hardly wait for the candles to be lighted. Daddy built a fire in the fireplace, and the tree twinkled in its corner.

The Frasers arrived first, Mr. Fraser carrying Susan, round-eyed at this novel nighttime outing. Ginnie greeted them at the door with her father.

"Hello, Susan," she cried, stooping to unbutton the child's coat as her father set her down. "Do you know what? We're going upstairs and play."

But Susan's eyes wandered with interest to the tree and the snapping fire. Here was something new added since her last excursion to Ginnie's house.

"Come on, honey." Ginnie held out her hand as the doorbell rang to announce the next guests.

"Here are her pajamas." Mrs. Fraser handed Ginnie a small bag.

Susan looked over her shoulder as Ginnie guided her upstairs. "We'll go in Ginnie's room."

Susan had a different idea. She put her hand on the attic door. "Up."

"Not tonight," Ginnie said hastily. "It's cold and dark up there. Come on in my room. And what do you think? You're going to stay here all night and sleep in this nice twin bed."

The sound of the doorbell reached Susan's ears and reminded her that interesting events were taking place below. "Down," she announced, marching toward the stairs.

Ginnie went after her. "I've got a wonderful idea.

Let's play you and Ginnie are going on a choo-choo, far, far away. We're going to sleep on the choo-choo." Susan looked interested, and Ginnie pressed her advantage. "This is the bed on the choo-choo. We're going to — Schenectady!"

Momentarily distracted, Susan forgot the goings on downstairs. "Here we are." Ginnie lifted her onto the bed. "We're going to Schenectady, and you have to get undressed, so that you can go to bed on the choo-choo."

Susan permitted Ginnie to slip off her small brown oxfords and socks and lifted her arms obediently to have her dress removed. Ginnie had her in miniature pink-flannel pajamas in a moment and slid her under the covers. "Now you're on your way to Schenectady. Isn't this fun?"

Her charge nodded assent.

This was going to be easy, Ginnie told herself. She lay down on her own bed. If Susan went right off to sleep she could go downstairs. She was eager to see the candles lighted and the beautiful food set out.

But her success was short-lived. Susan sat up and threw off the blanket. Ginnie sat up too. "Shall I tell you a story while we're on the train?" she asked hastily.

"Mrs. Bobbin," said Susan.

Ginnie had hoped that Mrs. Bobbin stayed home nights. "All right," she said patiently, as Susan presented her brow for the double knock. "Now Mrs. Bobbin can go to Schenectady," she suggested hopefully.

But Mrs. Bobbin was already sliding off the bed. "Down," she said firmly.

Because she was glad of an excuse to get downstairs herself, Ginnie decided that it would do no harm to take the child down for a minute. She looked so cute, with her pink cheeks and pink pajamas. But she bargained first. "If I take you down for a minute, Susan — I mean Mrs. Bobbin — then will Susan be a good girl and go to sleep?"

Mrs. Bobbin indicated that Susan would.

"Then come on, but don't forget."

Predinner conversation was gay in the living room, and Susan's appearance was greeted with admiring cries.

"Oh, no!" said Susan's father.

"It's all right for a couple of minutes," Ginnie heard Mrs. Fraser murmur to her husband. "Come on," she told her small daughter, "you may stay for a little while, and then you must go back upstairs with Ginnie." Susan — Mrs. Bobbin, that was —

snuggled happily into the chair with her mother and looked complacently on the party.

Ginnie slipped into the kitchen. Mother was just carrying the casserole of potatoes to the table. "See if your rolls are brown." Ginnie opened the oven door and took out the rolls, golden-crusted.

"Put them in the breadbasket." Mother was slipping out of her green tulle party apron.

The table was enchanting, delectable fare glistening in the candlelight. But as she placed the basket of rolls in place, Ginnie's attention was caught by conversation from the living room.

"Come on now, Susan," Mrs. Fraser was saying, "I'll take you upstairs."

There was no response. Ginnie, in the doorway, saw Susan avert a small determined face.

"This is a party for big people. Little girls must go to bed. It's late," Mrs. Fraser argued.

"Mrs. Bobbin," said Susan.

"You can't argue with her," said Mr. Fraser. "Just take her upstairs. I'll take her myself. Come on, Susan, we're going to bed!"

"No, no, no!" shrieked Susan, clutching her chair. "Mrs. Bobbin!"

"What does she mean, Mrs. Bobbin? I told you it wouldn't work, bringing her," her father said glumly.

"What do we do, have a scene in front of the company? Come on, Susan," he coaxed, getting hold of one hand, which she promptly wriggled away. "You're going to bed," Mr. Fraser announced, patience exhausted, and he picked up his child.

"Mrs. Bobbin!" shrieked Susan piteously, kicking. "Mrs. Bobbin, Mrs. Bobbin!"

Ginnie had stood fascinated by this display. Suddenly she came to her senses, remembered her role as baby-sitter, and hurried into the living room. "Oh, wait just a minute," she begged. She stood on tiptoe, tapped Susan's anguished forehead twice, and the screams subsided to small volcanic sobs.

"Now it's all right. Susan is back," Ginnie assured her soothingly. "Are you coming with Ginnie, so we can go on the choo-choo?"

The red-gold head nodded. Susan slipped from her father's lax arms to the floor and reached to take Ginnie's hand. With one final sniff and tears on her cheeks, she trotted from the room without a backward look, with the one person in the world who understood Mrs. Bobbin.

"Well, I'll be . . ." Ginnie heard Mr. Fraser say softly, as they climbed the stairs.

"Ginnie and her juniors!" Daddy remarked with a chuckle. Laughter rose then and drowned the rest of the comments.

Susan went to sleep happy, Ginnie's Teddy clutched tightly. Ginnie was able to slip back downstairs after a while.

There were compliments for her. "Did you make these wonderful rolls?" Mr. Olsen asked.

"They're heavenly!" Mrs. Sebring agreed.

"You can come and keep house for us any day," Mr. Fraser assured her. "Anybody who can make rolls like these and cast a spell over that imp . . ."

"I'll be over!" Ginnie assured him gaily.

It was two days later when Daddy finally got the car out of the garage and the chains on. "If I don't do some marketing we'll have to live without food," Mother said. "Are you coming to the store with us, Ginnie?"

Ginnie was having a good game of snowball with Peter. "No, thanks."

They stopped to rest after a while, sitting on Ginnie's front steps. "School on Monday," Peter said glumly.

Ginnie sighed. For a few days her thoughts had been caught up in the Christmas whirl and the blizzard and the supper party. Now the fun was all over. There was nothing much to look forward to but endless winter. Not even skating, she reflected, with the

pond covered deeply with snow. No nursery. . . .
She sat in silent gloom.

And in the silence she heard the telephone ring.
"I'll be right back," she told Peter, getting up.

"I have to go anyhow. See you," Peter said, and
departed.

It was Mrs. Fraser. "Oh, Ginnie," she said, "can
you sit with Susan this afternoon? I've simply got to
get to the store."

"Yes!" Ginnie cried.

"Can you come over here?"

"Over there?" She hadn't heard rightly, of course.
"You mean you want me to come over to your house
to sit?"

"Yes, honey, I do. Susan's daddy says any girl
who can handle Susan the way you did the other
night is old enough to stay here with her when I'm
out. I mentioned it to your mother, and she agreed."

"She did?" Ginnie's senses were reeling. "What
time shall I come?" she cried.

Susan was at the window, watching. Mrs. Fraser,
all ready to leave, opened the door. "Susan could
hardly wait," she said. "You know, Ginnie, you have
quite a talent with children."

She stood still. "Talent?"

"Yes, you have. Some people just seem to know how to manage children, others never do. 'By now.'" She waved to Susan. Ginnie held the door for her, closing it slowly.

Talent. She had a talent. She turned finally, still slightly dazed with the revelation, to the expectant Susan.

If the Frasers think I'm old enough to baby-sit, maybe other people will too, her mind was saying. And she thought quickly, Then it won't matter about the nursery, even if I don't have it again in the spring. Still, I *might* have it!

Because of the snow and the party, she had not seen Geneva since the day after Christmas. But there was news to impart now. The next day Ginnie started early. Geneva was out when she arrived — dog-walking, her mother said. She came in shortly, red-cheeked.

"Briskie just loves the snow," she announced. "He wallowed in it. Ginnie, know what?"

"What?"

"I think I'll be a veterinarian when I grow up."

"Good."

Geneva had pulled off her wet mittens and was tugging at her coat. "What are you going to be?" she inquired cheerfully, sitting down to remove her galoshes. "When you grow up?"

Ginnie gazed down at her, guarding for a little longer the wonderful secret that at last she had earned the right to be a full-fledged baby-sitter.

"Don't you know?" Geneva persisted, looking up.

Quite suddenly she did know. But when it slipped out it was so unexpected it surprised Ginnie herself. "Yes," she said slowly, "I know. I think I am just going to be — a mother!"